CW00732565

THE CURSE

OF CANNOW'S END

To Suzanne,
Enjoy the book!

By Ian Yearsley

Published by

MELROSE BOOKS

An Imprint of Melrose Press Limited
St Thomas Place, Ely
Cambridgeshire
CB7 4GG, UK
www.melrosebooks.co.uk

FIRST EDITION

Copyright © Ian Yearsley 2012

The Author asserts his moral right to
be identified as the author of this work

Cover designed by Catherine McIntyre

ISBN 978-1-908645-10-4

All rights reserved. No part of this publication may be reproduced, stored in a retrieval system, or transmitted, in any form or by any means electronic, mechanical, photocopying, recording or otherwise, without the prior permission of the publishers.

This book is sold subject to the condition that it shall not, by way of trade or otherwise, be lent, re-sold, hired out or otherwise circulated without the publisher's prior consent in any form of binding or cover other than that in which it is published and without a similar condition including this condition being imposed on the subsequent purchaser.

Printed and bound in Great Britain by:
Mimeo Ltd, Huntingdon, Cambridgeshire

FSC
www.fsc.org
MIX
From responsible
sources
FSC® C019549

This book is dedicated to my wife, Alison: thank you for proofreading the text for me and for providing some excellent ideas and feedback about the story.

This novel is entirely a work of fiction. The names, characters and incidents portrayed in it are the work of the author's imagination. Any resemblance to actual persons, living or dead, events or localities is entirely coincidental.

**Cutting from the *Thamesmouth Evening Star*,
Friday, 24th September:**

HUMAN HEAD FOUND
IN CHURCHYARD

Police have today launched a major murder inquiry after a human head was found in All Saints churchyard in the village of Cannow's End in south-east Essex.

The gruesome object, discovered this morning by a woman out walking her dog, has been removed from the site for forensic examination, but police presence at All Saints remains high and a cordon has been thrown around the churchyard to prevent the site from being disturbed. Exact details of the case remain sketchy as police try to play down the incident, but this newspaper has exclusively been able to piece together the sequence of events since this morning's discovery.

Cannow's End is a small hilltop village with an equally small and very insular community. The church stands at the remote western end of the village at the end of the High Street – one of only two roads which lead to the building, the other being Church Lane, the dead-end haunt of courting couples. The woman who found the object was walking her dog around the churchyard as usual at about seven o'clock this morning, enjoying her daily view of the River Crouch valley to the north, when the animal started barking and pawing excitedly at the base of a large bush growing beside the church tower. She went to see what the cause of the excitement was and found a head, thought to be that of an elderly male, lying on the ground.

She then ran screaming for help to the nearby rectory, which stands barely a hundred yards south of the churchyard. Reverend Susannah Black, the controversial new rector of All Saints, who was installed as incumbent just three days ago, immediately telephoned the police. The Chief Constable of South Anglia Police, Edward Glass, this afternoon praised Reverend Black for her calmness in dealing with such an unexpected and horrific situation.

The unnamed woman who found the head is said to be suffering from severe shock and is under heavy sedation at Thamesmouth Hospital. Police immediately cordoned off the churchyard and, after a detailed inspection *in situ*, the head was removed to secure premises for further forensic examination. A mobile police incident room has been set up in the High Street, outside the churchyard's eastern entrance.

Activities at the site have continued throughout the day, with news crews from local and national radio and TV stations arriving in droves late this afternoon as word of the incident spread. A police spokesman told us just before we went to press that it was too early to ascertain precisely what had happened, but that further information would be issued as soon as the results of their investigations had been obtained. He added that such a horrific discovery would seem to point to there being a murderer on the loose in the Cannow's End area, and warned all local residents to lock their doors and windows and be very vigilant for strangers in the area.

Reverend Black said that she hoped local people would

join with her in asking God to see that the murderer was brought to justice. She made an impassioned appeal to local residents and churchgoers to do all they could to help the police with their enquiries.

"I urge anyone who knows anything about this incident to contact the police immediately," she told us. "How such an appalling crime can have been committed at all, let alone in a churchyard in the sight of God, is beyond me."

Local residents were said to be extremely frightened by the whole affair. Pensioner Amelia Cartwright, 79, who lives in the first cottage on the south side of the High Street, right next door to the church, and is chairman of Cannow's End's Parochial Church Council, told us that she still could not believe that such an event had occurred almost literally on her doorstep.

"This whole episode has upset me greatly," she told us in a faltering voice. "Two nights ago all the Harvest Festival offerings were stolen from the church, and today there's a murderer on the loose. You just don't expect this sort of thing to happen here. Maybe in some of the larger nearby towns like Thamesmouth or London, but not in a little village like Cannow's End.

"I haven't felt as anxious about anything since those funny storms we had here at Candlemass – thunder, lightning, hurricane winds... The whole church was creaking then like it was alive. I'm surprised it didn't fall down!"

There has been an air of horror and disbelief in the village all day, and we urge all Cannow's End residents to watch TV news programmes this evening for further information. We will bring you an update on this story in a special Saturday edition tomorrow, available from usual *Star* outlets. For those unfamiliar with the village we have reproduced a map alongside this article, showing all the main Cannow's End landmarks.

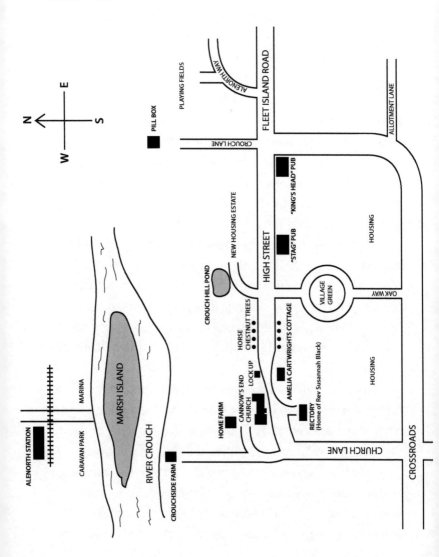

Extract from Stephen Varley's journal, Friday, 24th September:

6pm

I've just read tonight's Star, which the paperboy seemed to take an age to deliver, and can no longer pretend that what happened to me last night was a dream. I have been trying to put it out of my mind all day. I even avoided taking my usual walk up to the church today, just in case it was true. I haven't dared to leave the house all day. I planned to do some writing to take my mind off things, but I haven't been able to concentrate.

Miss Cartwright has just telephoned to say that she has called an emergency PCC meeting for tomorrow evening to discuss the situation. She has been trying to get information from the police about the incident, but is finding it difficult to get anything out of them. The churchyard is completely cordoned off and no one but the police have been allowed in all day. I didn't have the heart to tell her that I knew more than the police did about it.

She asked me if I'd seen anyone near the church when I was doing the rounds last night, but I didn't know what to say so I just said "No". I'm surprised she didn't see, or certainly hear, anything herself – but then she is going a bit deaf, I suppose, and she does like the sherry! Thank God it's so much easier to lie to someone over the phone than it is face to face!

I really don't know what to do next. I am petrified about what happened but am too scared to say anything to anyone in case they think I am mad. The police think they are looking for a murderer, but I fear they are sadly mistaken. What I saw last night has convinced me once and for all that things are not as they seem in this village. I'm beginning to wish I had never come here. I must try to pluck up the courage to tell someone about it before things get completely out of hand. Maybe at the PCC meeting tomorrow night? I'm just a bit worried that they might dismiss me as a crank...

Cutting from the *Thamesmouth Evening Star*,

Special Weekend Edition,

Saturday, 25th September:

HEAD BELONGS TO REVEREND PARK

Incredible rumours were circulating today that the human head discovered at All Saints churchyard in Cannow's End yesterday morning belongs to the recently deceased rector of Cannow's End, 77-year-old Reverend Alfred Park. Local police officers have apparently been claiming since yesterday that the badly damaged facial features resembled those of Reverend Park, long-serving rector of All Saints, who died on September 14th.

This latest twist to the affair now casts doubt on the 'murderer-at-large' theory which seemed the most obvious scenario when we went to press yesterday, but senior officers will clearly want to be sure of their facts before making any definitive statement about this incredible claim.

Reverend Park, rector of All Saints for thirty-seven years until his death just over a week ago, was buried in the churchyard on September 21st, the same day that his successor, Reverend Susannah Black, was inaugurated. Reverend Park was much respected throughout the community. It is believed that he was the last surviving member of an old Cannow's End family, and he was buried in the family's plot on the north side of the church, where most of the graves in the churchyard are located. His funeral was attended by hundreds of mourners and was given generous press coverage by this newspaper. His grave, which is believed to have been greatly disturbed, has today been the focus of police attention, with the media and a growing band of sightseers being kept well away from the site.

It seems incredible to speculate that police will indeed conclude that the head belongs to Reverend Park. If they do, they will surely be expected to give a full explanation of the circumstances leading up to its discovery, and a credible explanation of how it came to be there in the first place. Who on earth would want to dig up the grave of such a well-respected man as Alfred Park?

Local people we spoke to this afternoon for this special Saturday edition of the *Star* – a unique achievement in our long and illustrious publishing history – were already dismissing the claims that the head belonged to the former rector. How, they asked, could it possibly be? Reverend Park has been buried for only four days, and everyone we spoke to was either present at his funeral or knew someone who was. We have to admit that we are inclined to share their disbelief.

NB We regret that we are unable to produce a paper tomorrow (Sunday), but will update you fully on the developments at Cannow's End in Monday's edition.

Extract from the blog of Michael Swain, aged 16, posted on the Internet on Saturday, 25th September at 3.07 p.m.

me 18 year old brother keith and me went up canowsend church on friday cos we heard sumthing woz goin on and there woz sum kind of murder or sumthing up there! the coppers were there and they were like u cant cum in here! and we were like it's a public church an we can fuckin cum up here if we want to! and they were like not today sunshine unless u want 2 go up the nick! omg! so we were like ok we'll cum back sum other time then! and we went back 2 keith's car where we left it in church lane.

i bought the star on the way home and fuck me they found a head up there! we thought we'd try 2 go bak at nite but the coppers were still there and had it all fenced off and stuff. we took stripe my dalmation with us and omg his frikkin ears were sticking up on his head and his hackles were up on his back like he'd seen a ghost and he kept looking and growling at sum big bildin just south of the church. keith says it woz the rectory where the vicar lives. we went down the road a bit away from the coppers and i held stripe back while keith crept thru the bushes 2 c if anyfing woz goin on in there. he's crept about up here in the dark b4 like last year on halloween but this woz my first time an i woz a bit spooked by the dark an stuff! he sed there were 2 or 3 figurs silhouetted aginst sum candles in an upstairs bedroom on the south side of the rectory away from the church an i woz like wot aint they got any fuckin electric? the fukkin streetlites are working! and we were like there mus be sumfing dodgy goin on.

we plan 2 go back there 2nite for another look.

**Extract from the minute book of the Parochial
Church Council of All Saints church, Cannow's End,
emergency meeting called by the chairman,
Miss Amelia Cartwright, Saturday,
25th September at 6.00 p.m.**

1. *Miss Cartwright welcomed the new rector, Rev
Susannah Black, to her first meeting and expressed
her sadness that it could not have been under more
joyous circumstances.*

2. *Incident at All Saints*
*Miss Cartwright asked for it to be minuted that she
had called this emergency meeting as soon as possible after what she thought was the 'murder' at All
Saints churchyard because she wanted to obtain the
views of PCC members and present a cohesive view
to the press, etc. The PCC was widely respected in the
village and would be looked to for information and
reassurance.*

*Speculation in this evening's special edition of the
Thamesmouth Evening Star seemed to be implying,
however, that there was not, in fact, a murderer
at large, but their alternative theory was far too
horrific for members to contemplate.*

*Mr. Varley confirmed that he had been up to the
church quite late on the night before the 'incident'
(Thursday 23rd) in case the thieves who had stolen*

the Harvest Festival offerings the previous evening were intending to come back for something more valuable. He reminded members that he had adopted a similar approach in May when the church was vandalised, but had met with a similar lack of success in tracing the perpetrators of the crime. He could not remember what time he had been at the building but he said he thought it was probably around 11 o'clock. In response to questions Mr. Varley said that he had not yet volunteered this information to the police, largely because he felt it was not relevant to their investigations. Fellow PCC members urged Mr. Varley to consider speaking to them as soon as possible.

Miss Cartwright said that she thought she had heard some strange noises at the church on Thursday round about midnight, but stressed that she had been having increasing difficulty with her hearing of late and often heard high-pitched whines and the like, which were simply the wind whistling through the church tower. She had been interviewed by the police herself, but had been unable to tell them anything more than she was now telling members. Neither had she been able to obtain any information from them about the specific details of the case.

Reverend Black said she had gone to bed early on Thursday, had slept very soundly all night, and had not heard or seen anything. Mr. Varley confirmed that the lights had been off at the rectory when he had entered the churchyard. Reverend Black had also been interviewed by police officers, but had similarly not been able to shed any light on the matter.

No one else had been at the church on the 23rd.

Miss Cartwright impressed upon Mr. Varley the urgent need she felt for him to speak to the police as he was the most likely person to be of any help to their enquiries. It was agreed that Mr. Varley should further liaise with the police on behalf of the PCC if required, as Miss Cartwright's deputy.

Miss Cartwright closed the discussion with an expression of hope that the matter would soon be resolved and forgotten. Reverend Black seconded that view.

3. Any Other Business

One other item of business was taken whilst members were all together, during which it was agreed to call a halt to the investigations into humane ways of killing the pigeons which had been infesting the church tower throughout the summer, as the numbers of birds living there had declined dramatically in recent months to more manageable numbers, possibly due to the unseasonably cold August weather.

Extract from Stephen Varley's journal,
Saturday, 25th September:

8:30pm

The PCC meeting went OK, but I really felt a bit awkward about saying too much and I think Miss Cartwright suspects I know more than I was letting on. She might be going deaf, but she's still a shrewd old bird! I have to say I'm still not sure about Reverend Black… I think my first impressions of her were correct. I can't quite put my finger on it, but there's something about her that makes me uneasy.

And as for the lovely Sophie, the world's most beautiful minutes' secretary, I'm still struggling to cope with being in the same room as her, to be honest! I don't know what it is but whenever I set eyes on her my heart starts pounding in my chest, and I can feel myself blushing and getting flustered. She moves like an angel and her voice drives me to distraction. I've never really recovered from her first meeting in June, when I suddenly caught myself staring at her and had to look away quickly when she glanced unexpectedly over towards me. I know I blushed then when she smiled at me in response. I thought I'd got away with the whole thing, but tonight during the break when I was serving the tea and biscuits I became all flustered when it was time to serve her, and I accidentally tipped a plate of biscuits onto her lap! She stood up suddenly with an almost automatic reaction, and the biscuits and plate all clattered to the floor. They made a hell of a noise! Her eyes momentarily flashed anger at me, and I was very apologetic. She seemed to have calmed down by the end of the evening; I think she was more embarrassed by the commotion created and by being the centre of attention when everyone looked round than by the actual incident. Get your act together, Stephen! If you're in a state like that every time you're in the same room as her, you might scare her off of coming to future meetings!

Anyway, on the way back from tonight's meeting I stopped off at the church. There were a lot of people up there – police, press and members of the public. I hung around for a while outside the mobile incident room the police have set up in the High Street – it looks like one of those old prefabricated class-rooms we used to have at school. I almost went in to speak to them, but there was too much of a commotion going on for me to think things through properly, so I used that as an excuse to come home. Where is Mr. Courage when I need him?!

I really am quite troubled about this whole affair. Alf was the only person I really knew well enough in this whole community to talk to about such an important thing, and he's no longer with us. In the few months I've been here since the start of the year I've tried to get involved in things and to meet people, but it's difficult for an outsider to be accepted in such an insular community as this. If you don't have a Cannow's End pedigree going back to at least the 17th century it's as if you've got some kind of black mark against you! A stain on your character! At least with Alf I knew him a bit before I moved here, if only by reputation, and he did his best to make me feel welcome. My parents always said he had been a good friend to them and I could rest assured that he would be the same to me. Well he was, but it's just that sometimes I wish I'd bought that flat in Thamesmouth a minute's walk from the station, with Boots and Debenhams and HMV all to hand. I would still have had a new house and new town to get accustomed to, but at least the community there would've been a bit more tuned in to the modern world! I don't like change at all really – probably typical of the English in that respect – and I suppose I moved to Cannow's End in the end partly because I'd heard of Alf and partly because the estate agent had described it as a "delightful little village, with a long and interesting history" and it just sounded ideal for me to relax here and write my novel. And anyway, why live in the town when you can live in the country? I also had this vague feeling that the village was somehow calling me to it – some kind of predestined course I was to embark upon. It was Alf who suggested I get involved with him and the PCC to get to know a few people here, and the rest, as they say, is history!

Anyway, some course I've embarked upon! The trouble with being the youngest person on the committee (33 this year, thank you very much!) is that you feel a certain responsibility for looking after everything – the older ones, well-meaning though they are, just don't have the get-up-and-go! And as for checking the church for vandals at night, they're all a bit too old and frail for that, apart from the beautiful Sophie, who's 34 I think, but we can't have that angel roaming around alone in the dark! Not sure about Reverend Black – I think she's probably in her early 50s.

This whole business has been a complete nightmare for me, and I'm going to have to tell someone about it soon. I think I'll try to sleep on it and think about what to do in the morning – not that I'll sleep very well if last night is anything to go by. I still feel a bit run down from Thursday night's exertions, and I only hope I can actually get some sleep tonight!

Extract from the blog of Michael Swain, posted on the Internet on Sunday,

26th September at 2.01 a.m.

well we went up canowsend again 2nite as planned and parked at the bottom of church lane well away from the coppers. i've just got in so i thought i'd update u.

we didn't take stripe this time cos we thought he'd bark 2 much and the coppers would hear. i wanted 2 take him but keith said no. we crept thru the hedge again and i got branches sticking in my ear in the dark! lol. all the lites were off at the rectory this time so we stayed at the edge of the garden and close 2 the road. keith suddenly said can u here sum hi pitched droning noise or sumfing like monks chanting in victorian times and stuff and i woz like no i can't hear anyfing. wot u fuckin talking about? and he said listen properly! and i woz like well i can here sumfing but i wouldn't say it woz monks. wot would they be doin here?

then keith said we need 2 get closer, so we crept thru the dark 2wards the building. i got scratched by sum fuckin bush on my face and let out a yell. keith sed sumfing like shut up u idiot and keep your fuckin noise down and i woz like sorry and that but i couldn't help it!

we reachd the corner of the building and there woz defnitely sum noise coming from inside.

keith sed thats munks an im like it sownds more like granny's relaxashun cd thats got red indian chantin on lol! we crept up 2 the window and tried 2 peer in but the curtains woz drawn. we crept along in the dark 2 the next window, me followin keith cos he ad dun this b4 an i adnt, and i woz like this is a bit dark, how the fuck can u c where you're goin? the curtains woz drawn in the secund window 2 so we woz jus gonna try a third 1 wen i fell over sum flowerpot or sumfing that sum stupid old bat had left in the way and made a hell of a racket! a lite came on in the howse and i cud c keith's face in the dark 4 the first time and he dint luk none 2 pleased wiv me! u dickhead e says an slaps me rownd the head an disappears off in2 the dark bak 2wards the road where we came from. i cud hear sum1 fumblin at the door so im like omg im fucking outta here an i ran off after him!

we ran down 2 the car an got in an sped off an the first thing i did woz cum in an rite this up. keith says i cant go wiv him agin unless i can be more quiet. e says read sum detective novels an c how they creep about an copy them so ill read 1 of me old man's ones 2morrow.

Extract from the report of Scenes of Crime officers to the Detective Chief Inspector in charge of the so-called 'Severed Head' case at Cannow's End, Sunday, 26th September:

We have examined as requested the area around the grave of the late Reverend Alfred Park at All Saints church, Cannow's End, Essex in connection with what the tabloids are calling the 'Severed Head' case, and wish to report the findings below.

There is most definitely evidence that Reverend Park's grave has been disturbed, but we are unclear as to the precise cause of this disturbance. The many wreaths and floral tributes which had been placed on the grave at the time of burial were found upon initial inspection to be lying haphazardly around it and the earth which was used to fill the grave has been greatly disturbed – a hole of about 12-18 inches in diameter has been dug into the grave from the surface at the headstone (western) end. The gravedigger has told us that the grave was filled with earth immediately after the funeral and that the wreaths from the many well-wishers were placed on top. He saw the grave still in this condition on the afternoon of the 23rd September, two days after the funeral.

As to clues about the cause of the disturbance, we must confess to being somewhat baffled so far. There are what appear to be animal footprints and claw marks in the earth around the grave and it would seem likely that the hole down into it was dug by some kind of animal, perhaps a dog or a fox. The marks are regrettably not sufficiently clear to allow us to precisely identify the species of animal in question. The clarity of the prints is such as to imply a scuffle around the head end of the grave – next to the headstone, where the hole has been dug – perhaps between two or three largish animals. We have taken advice from police dog handlers as well as from a local vet and a keeper from Thamesmouth Zoo, and the best we can say is that it looks as if two large dogs have been fighting on the grave. It seems likely that one of them then proceeded to dig into the grave, perhaps excited by the smells emanating from it, which the disturbance to the earth caused by the fighting enabled to come to the surface.

Of particular concern to this investigation is additional evidence that splinters of oak planks have been found both on and in the vicinity of the grave. The undertaker who handled Reverend Park's funeral has confirmed to us that this wood was used in the construction of his coffin, which was paid for by the many generous donations to the rector's memory which came from members of his congregation. Similar splinters were found by the bush where the head was discovered.

We have therefore regrettably to conclude from the evidence to hand that it is indeed possible to believe that the head discovered at All Saints on the morning of the 24th September is that of the late rector, the Reverend Alfred Park. We are arranging for formal identification to take place later today. The cause of the head's exhumation seems, as we have said above, most likely to be dogs digging up the grave, much in the manner that they are known to look for buried bones, and removing the head to the location where it was found. This explanation is clearly not entirely satisfactory, however, as it leaves a lot of questions unanswered. These questions would have to include:

- Would a dog really dig down six feet, chew up a coffin lid and remove the human head contained in the coffin to another location?

- Would a dog in any case even have the physical strength do this? (The handlers we spoke to were very sceptical about a dog having strong enough teeth and jaws to chew through the wood, even if one had dug down through six feet of earth.) And:
- If a dog was not responsible, then was some other animal perhaps involved?

These questions lead us to speculate further that if dogs *were* involved, then there may well have been some human involvement as well, perhaps in exercising control of the dogs and perhaps even in specifically targeting Reverend Park's grave. You will be aware that the Harvest Festival food that villagers had collected was stolen from All Saints two days before the head was found, and that the building suffered some vandalism in the summer. Perhaps someone has a vendetta against the church? There are plenty of human footprints to examine around the grave but the disturbance to the earth is such that it is not possible to tell which of them originates from the date of the funeral, and which is of more recent date.

Another possible option for these investigations is that *only* human beings were involved in the head's exhumation (two or three appropriately equipped men would collectively seem to be capable of carrying out the task in the manner described) and that the dog fight took place independently, the animals being attracted to the location by the smells emanating from the newly disturbed grave. (The animal footprints are more recent than the human ones.) The style of digging looks more like animal than man, however. Furthermore, if the head is that of Reverend Park, it remains conjecture as to why a person (or persons) should want to go to so much trouble to exhume the head and then simply leave it where they did.

Taking all the above points into account we have to conclude that this is clearly NOT a murder case, as the 'victim', if it is Reverend Park, was already dead at the time of disturbance; but the person or persons responsible for this atrocity must be considered to be very dangerous to ordinary members of the public, and we would advise careful handling of the case where the media and the general public (particularly the local villagers, who held Reverend Park in high esteem) are concerned.

If dogs and/or humans were not involved (which must be extremely unlikely) then perhaps some wild animal living on the marshes near the river or in one of the many copses hereabouts was responsible. If that were the case, and we are preparing to take formal advice on this from local experts, we would still feel inclined to ask numerous questions before being entirely satisfied with our conclusions, and we have to admit that we do not believe that we have the answers to those questions to hand at the present time.

We are aware of the results of the forensic examination of the head itself and the complementary views of local officers that it belongs to Reverend Park. This would be entirely consistent with our own findings (which are by no means perfect) and we support wholeheartedly Forensic's recommendation that Reverend Park's grave should be reopened for further examination. At the very least, this would put at rest the minds of local residents, whose close-knit community has clearly been horrified by this incident, and would obviously allow us to carry out further investigations into the details of the incident. It would be well to remember that many of the villagers were devoted members of Reverend Park's congregation and, whether we like it or not, we will not be able to keep these discoveries under wraps for very long.

In summary, we regret that we will be unable to bring this case to a satisfactory conclusion without further significant evidence. This is a case unlike any that we have previously encountered, and we look forward to receiving formal permission for the grave to be reopened, with the hope of shedding further light on the details of the matter in the not-too-distant future.

**E-mail to The Chief Constable of South Anglia Police,
Edward Glass, from the Detective Chief Inspector
in charge of the police incident room,
Cannow's End High Street,
Sunday, 26ᵗʰ September, 3.30 p.m.:**

Sir,

We have been handed a letter from a Cannow's End resident, Mr. Stephen Varley, who says that he may have some
information about the 'Severed Head' case and would like
to meet you in person to discuss the matter. Several things
he said implied to us that he genuinely did know something,
but he was reluctant to speak to anyone but you. He says
you are a friend of his parents – David and Stella Varley – and
has given us a telephone number and address at which to
contact him.

Mr. Varley was very nervous when talking to us, Sir, and
we suggest you endeavour to speak to him at the earliest
available opportunity.

DCI Rogers, Cannow's End Incident Room

Cutting from the *Thamesmouth Evening Star*, Monday, 27th September:

SEVERED HEAD CASE:
INVESTIGATIONS CONTINUE

Police were today staying tight lipped about their investigations into the 'Severed Head' case at All Saints church in Cannow's End, where an initial examination of former rector Reverend Alfred Park's grave has now been concluded.

Scenes of Crime officers were clearly uneasy about revealing too many details of their findings to the media and, for the first time since the case began, retired to their incident room without making a formal statement to waiting reporters. This approach has fuelled speculation that they are about to announce that they will be reopening Reverend Park's grave to establish once and for all that the head found at All Saints three days ago does indeed belong to the former rector.

Access to the church is still barred to the media and to the growing band of sightseers, several hundred of whom were present at All Saints today. Such is the interest that the case has generated that extra police officers have been drafted in to prevent any encroachment into the churchyard.

The still relatively new incumbent, Reverend Susannah Black, told us that she has been fielding questions from newsmen all day and has been praying alone in the church on behalf of the village for a speedy outcome to police enquiries. Only a handful of church people have been allowed inside the police cordon since it was first erected and then only into the church building itself. The Bishop of South Anglia, paying a special visit to All Saints as a direct result of this case, was amongst those allowed in. The cancellation of yesterday's Harvest Festival service has added to the mood of despondency in the village, and the Bishop is obviously keen to provide spiritual guidance in person at this time of need. Police investigations at the bush where the head was discovered appear to be complete, and it now seems likely that the church building and at least part of the churchyard will be reopened for worship within the next few days. Reverend Black is preparing a special prayer for police investigators, the soul of Reverend Park and the 'criminal or criminals who perpetrated this vile crime', which will be read at the first service after the reopening of the church.

Needless to say, the local community is still in deep shock about the incident.

Note pushed through Stephen Varley's door on the evening of Monday, 27th September:

Dear Mr. Varley,

I have spoken to Mr. Glass, the Chief Constable, and he has agreed to speak to you in person as requested. He is coming to Cannow's End first thing tomorrow morning. I should be grateful if you would make yourself available to discuss the matter with him.

DCI Rogers, Cannow's End Incident Room

Transcript of a story on *South Anglia TV News*,

Monday, 27th September:

Police investigating the so-called 'Severed Head' case at Cannow's End in Essex have announced within the past hour that they have obtained permission to reopen the grave of a former rector there.

The Reverend Alfred Park died of natural causes on September 14th after over thirty years' service and was buried at All Saints church seven days later. A head found in the churchyard three days ago is widely believed to be that of the former rector.

Norman Parker has this report:

"The Chief Constable of South Anglia Police, Edward Glass, who is personally leading the police investigations, told a hastily convened and rather cramped press conference at Thamesmouth Police Station barely half an hour ago that permission to reopen Reverend Park's grave had been granted late this afternoon, following the recommendations of both forensic experts and Scenes of Crime officers. He also expressed his annoyance at 'the sensational way' in which the local media have reported the case.

"The local evening paper was claiming this afternoon that the grave would have to be reopened and the pressure of media attention at the police incident room in Cannow's End High Street has evidently prompted senior officers to make a statement to newsmen this evening.

"The head, whose discovery sparked off this extraordinary case, was found under a bush in the churchyard on Friday morning, and it is believed that investigations at the graveside have revealed unexplained signs of disturbance there.

"When pressed to say whether he thought the head did indeed belong to Reverend Park, Mr. Glass said that he was keeping an open mind about the matter, but that he had 'very good reason to believe' that it could be that of the former rector. The grave is expected to be reopened first thing tomorrow morning.

"The village of Cannow's End is home to a small, close-knit community of fewer than 2,000 inhabitants, not used to being the focus of national media attention. Historically a farming community, the village retains a distinct identity, and the horrific nature of this case has hit these people hard. With the grave of one of their much-loved former rectors about to be reopened, the atmosphere in the village tonight is electric and this whole community, like much of the country, is holding its breath.

"Norman Parker, South Anglia News, Thamesmouth Police Station, Essex."

Extract from the blog of Michael Swain, posted on the Internet on Monday, 27ᵗʰ September at 10.40 p.m.

well i read the star tonite an have jus seen the tv news an im findin it all bloody spooky! who wud dig up a vicar's head? omg! i spoke 2 keith abowt it an he seems 2 fink its sum people up 2 sum sort of ritual especiallly as there woz munks or sumfing in the rectory the uvver nite. he sed we shud go up the library and see if we can find out more.

we fownd a book abowt canowsend and its church which im reading while im typin this. ill let u no wots in it when ive read it. lol!

Extract from *A Guide to Cannow's End and its Church*, as found by Michael Swain at Thamesmouth public library:

The ancient hilltop village of Cannow's End probably gets its name from Saxon settlers in the 6th century. The name derives from the personal name of 'Cana', probably a local tribal leader. The hill on which the village stands offers good views over the surrounding countryside towards Thamesmouth to the south, and the beautiful valley of the River Crouch to the north.

The church of All Saints owes its magnificent stone tower to King Henry V, who is said to have built it in commemoration of a victory in battle. The tower is a significant landmark in this part of Essex and was used in the olden days as a beacon and a watchtower.

The current population of Cannow's End, no more than 2,000, is nonetheless the largest to date in the village's long and interesting history, and there are many families still living here who can trace their ancestry in the village for many generations back.

Cannow's End has many well-established traditions, amongst them that of a village of smugglers, though this pastime has long since died out. It also possesses an even older tradition as a village of witchcraft and the supernatural. Rowdy Halloween revellers are annual, if unwelcome, visitors to the village even to this day, mistakenly believing that these ancient beliefs have a basis in fact.

An 'olde worlde' village with a picturesque high street of ancient cottages, low-ceilinged pubs, and a proximity to the river and countryside, which only adds to its charm, Cannow's End is a popular haunt for ramblers and photographers. Nevertheless, it is a surprisingly quiet village – some might say eerily so – even at weekends.

The church of All Saints, which stands at the extreme western end of the village at the top of the High Street, is the oldest building in Cannow's End, parts of it dating from the 14th century. The massive west tower, however, like much of the rest of the building, belongs to the following century and rises to a height of about eighty feet. It is built of ragstone blocks, carried by river from quarries near Maidstone in Kent. The small porch is of much historical interest, while the grotesque gargoyle carvings on the waterspouts are important, if somewhat frightening-looking, architectural features.

Just outside the eastern end of the church, where the High Street ends, is a small village lock-up, dating from c.1775. Limited parking is available at the western end of the churchyard, which is fed by the only other access road, Church Lane, which leads up the hill from the crossroads.

A plan of the church is included in this guidebook to enable visitors to explore the building. Visitors are asked to respect this place of worship and offer a prayer to the Lord before they leave.

PLAN OF CANNOW'S END CHURCH

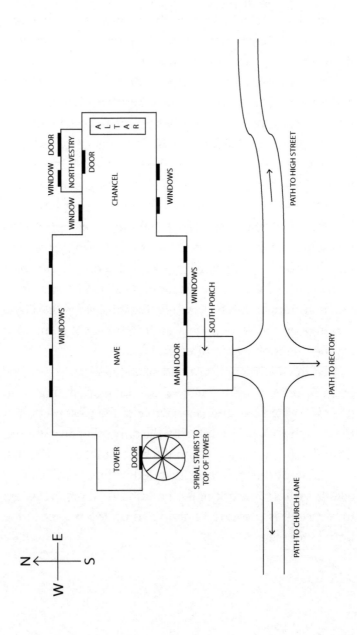

**Cutting from the *Thamesmouth Evening Star*,
Monday, 2nd February, pasted into Stephen Varley's
journal and shown to Mr. Edward Glass,
Chief Constable of South Anglia Police,
on Tuesday, 28th September:**

FREAK WEATHER CONTINUES

South-east Essex took another buffeting from the winds today as the freak weather conditions which have been affecting this area over the past two weeks showed no signs of abating.

Five boats were sunk and two others damaged at the Marsh Marina behind Marsh Island in the River Crouch as ferocious winds, reminiscent of those in the legendary 1987 'hurricane', tore the vessels from their moorings and smashed them against the yacht club jetty. Scores of trees in the Cannow's End and Pockingham areas were blown down, and emergency services have been inundated with requests for help with moving them. Roof tiles and windows have also been damaged by the winds.

Weather experts still seem unable to explain the cause of these curiously localised climatic conditions, which have seen the Crouch Valley and the villages to the north of Thamesmouth plagued by extreme conditions of torrential rainfall, tropical temperatures and magnificent thunderstorms, all within a matter of days. Conditions have changed dramatically, sometimes almost hourly, over the past few weeks, and there is a strange humidity in the air.

In Cannow's End, for example, which last week was cut off for twenty-four hours by flash floods on the low-lying land around the hilltop village, the atmosphere when the wind drops is balmy and oppressive. Locals seem as bemused by the conditions as we all are, and have been warned by weathermen to prepare for severe gales tonight and not to venture out after dark.

Extract from Stephen Varley's journal, Tuesday, 3rd February shown to Mr. Edward Glass, Chief Constable of South Anglia Police, on Tuesday, 28th September:

7am

Well, I've made it through to morning and the house is still intact. In fact, if anything the winds are dying down now and appear to be past their worst. If this keeps up, I'll venture up to the church later and see if there's any damage there. I haven't been out of the house for a couple of days with all this funny weather about, and I'm starting to run out of supplies. All Saints is in a rather exposed and susceptible position where the weather is concerned as the prevailing south-westerly wind whips up the slope across the fields and smacks straight into the upright tower. Still, the old girl's stood there for several hundred years now, and there can't be anything worse about this storm than any previous ones.

At least confinement to the house has enabled me to pick up this journal. I didn't fill it out much in January, what with moving house and settling in. I've always enjoyed keeping a journal though – you tend to forget all the things you've done and keeping a journal enables you to look back over your life and achievements: You never know how useful it will be. Hopefully, someone will look at this one day and read about how ferocious the weather conditions have been of late. They haven't been as strange as this for as long as I can remember.

Anyway, breakfast first, and then off to All Saints. No doubt our rector will be there before me. He's been really friendly and helpful in easing the process for me settling into the village and has even talked me into filling the vacancy on the PCC. Good old Alf!

2pm

I've just got back from the church and, as predicted, Alf was there already. The weather has definitely improved: The wind has stopped and the oppressive atmosphere that's been hovering over the village of late has lifted – just like the freshness you get after a heavy rainfall.

I'm pleased to say that the church building seems to be OK. A number of slates have been dislodged, which muggins here will no doubt have to replace (I can't see Miss Cartwright or the other pensioners climbing up a ladder), and one of the horse chestnut trees in the High Street has fallen into the street, but fortunately without making contact with any buildings.

There were a lot of people about in the village – all checking their properties and possessions to see if any damage had been done to them, and gossiping about the storms. The High Street was full of tree branches and bits of roof tile. My own house seems to have survived unscathed, I'm pleased to say.

Alf told me that Miss Cartwright heard a lot of strange noises in the churchyard during the night which kept her awake with worry. He told her it was only the wind, but he said that she seemed strangely unconvinced. The church was creaking and groaning like it was alive, she said – but there's so little damage there that I find that hard to believe. She also claimed to have seen a large animal scampering around by the lock-up

– probably a badger caught out in the winds. Maybe she's going senile as well as deaf!

I spoke to Alf about the Candlemass service at the weekend.

Extract from the annual report of the *South Anglia Wildlife Group Magazine*, *spring issue*, shown by Stephen Varley to Mr. Edward Glass, Chief Constable of South Anglia Police, on Tuesday, September 28th:

SQUIRREL NUMBERS FALLING

A sharp decline in squirrel numbers in south-east Essex is the most worrying statistic to be revealed by this year's annual mammal survey. Figures had been holding steady across the county for several years, but an alarming drop in numbers in the south-east has contributed to a reduction of the squirrel population by some 8.9 per cent over the past twelve months.

The woods around Bashingham and Cannow's End seem to have been particularly badly hit, with an analysis of the monthly statistics which are used to make up the annual total suggesting that December and January (usually a good month to see the animals) were the worst this year for squirrel sightings.

The reason for this sharp decline in numbers is unclear. Although Cannow's End and Bashingham are fairly urbanised communities there is an abundance of woodland in the area, and proximity to human-occupied areas is something on which squirrels normally thrive. Two new housing developments have been started in Cannow's End since last year's survey, but they are not in themselves sufficiently damaging to the woodland environment to be major causes of such a dramatic decline.

The fact that December and January show the largest annual reductions seems to point to a higher than usual death rate as winter began to make itself felt, but the drop in numbers is not matched by the numbers of carcasses found by survey recorders. Contrary to popular opinion, squirrels do not hibernate but, even so, a bad summer is more usually a killer of squirrels than a bad winter. Sources suggest that sufficient food was available in summer and autumn last year to have seen them through the winter.

The most likely cause of the reduction in numbers is thought to be a new strain of illness which has developed in the Cannow's End area, affecting the local squirrel population but as yet not spreading to squirrel communities elsewhere. Two badly mutilated carcasses were found in All Saints churchyard in March, and it is thought that a disease related to the killer bug *necrotising fasciitis* may be responsible.

Usual squirrel diseases such as *coccidiosis* (an enteritic disease) and *parapoxvirus* (rather like *myxamatosis*) would not cause such mutilation. Squirrels have no natural predators in the UK (unless one counts the pine marten), so it is unlikely that the specimens concerned were attacked by other animals.

Observations at the Cannow's End site are continuing, and tests will be carried out on all carcasses located. The Group would welcome any information that readers have on this situation.

**Cutting from the *Thamesmouth Evening Star*,
Monday, 3rd May, pasted into Stephen Varley's
journal and shown to Mr. Edward Glass,
Chief Constable of South Anglia Police,
on Tuesday, 28th September:**

CANNOW'S END CHURCH VANDALISED

Vandals broke into All Saints Church, Cannow's End, on Saturday night and caused several hundred pounds worth of damage to the building's interior.

Most of the damage was done in the vestry area, leading police to think that those responsible originally entered the church looking for valuables to steal. The electricity control panel was smashed, and none of the appliances in the building are now working. Nothing was taken except for two apples left in the vestry by the rector, which have disappeared, apparently eaten by the vandals.

It is widely thought that the culprits – probably teenagers – live in the village, as it is well-known locally that the church building is kept open. Reverend Alfred Park, rector of All Saints, is keen for the 'House of God' to be accessible to worshippers at all times.

Police enquiries into the incident continue.

Extract from Stephen Varley's journal, Tuesday, 4th May, shown to Mr. Edward Glass, Chief Constable of South Anglia Police, on Tuesday, 28th September:

8pm

I've just got back from making some repairs to the church roof, where a really strange thing happened to me.

I was up the ladder, having finally got round to replacing slates on the roof that were blown down in the February gales – a job I had been doing all afternoon and was determined to complete in one sitting. The light was fading fast as I finished the final slate and when coming back down the ladder I missed my step, lost my footing and only managed to prevent myself from falling by grabbing onto one of the gargoyle waterspouts on the porch for support. It felt really loose, as if it could be pulled out of the wall quite freely. I looked at it closely and the last rays of sunset reflected off my hammer onto the grotesque facial features, making the eye seem to wink at me as if the creature was alive. It gave me quite a nasty shock and I grabbed onto the ladder again and continued to make my way down, rather shaken. I knew I was tiring myself out in my keenness to finish the roof off, but I never expected to be so tired that I would start imagining things!

I actually spent the whole day at the church as it happens. Before doing the roof I fixed up the mess in the vestry that the vandals made on Saturday night when they took Alf's apples. I had a go with the electricity but I'm not too hot on that subject and had to retire defeated. I'll speak to Amelia about getting an electrician in.

I concur with the police view that the individuals involved were thieves looking for something to steal, who found nothing and smashed up the vestry in frustration. There were a couple of minor bits of damage in the nave, en route from the vestry to the main door, which appeared to have been caused by the vandals on their way out of the building through the main door – but the rest of the church interior was intact.

There was no damage to the exterior structure, though the ivy that was growing up the south wall next to the main door had been ripped off and thrown in a heap on the path – more signs of frustration, I suppose. This had caused some small pieces of masonry to become dislodged from approximately in the vicinity of the gargoyle waterspout mentioned above, which I suppose must explain why that object felt loose.

What with storms, strange noises and vandals, it's not been a vintage year for All Saints so far – or for me! So much for coming to a 'quiet rural village' for relaxation – I've had hardly any time to get on with my novel so far, which was the principal purpose of me coming here. Alf will not hear of the building being closed though. "If you can't leave a church open, what can you leave?" he says. "There must be something seriously wrong with our society if it comes to that." I have to agree.

I did, however, get him to agree that we should keep a close eye on things for a while: we don't want those would-be thieves coming back and doing some more damage. I've decided to have a look round after dark periodically to make sure that everything is OK. I'll do the same every night for the next few weeks until I'm happy that things have quietened down.

**Extract from Stephen Varley's journal,
Tuesday, 22ⁿᵈ June, shown to Mr. Edward Glass,
Chief Constable of South Anglia Police,
on Tuesday, 28ᵗʰ September:**

1am

Bloody Hell! I don't normally swear but I'm shaking like a leaf with fright and it's as much as I can do to write properly at the moment.

I went up to the church at about 11:30pm to make sure everything was OK. I've been 'doing my rounds' like this for about eight weeks now, since the vandalism incident on the night of 1ˢᵗ May. I've become a bit obsessed with it and can't let it go even though nothing more has happened in the interim. I suppose it's a bit like stopping doing the Lottery – you're too scared to do it in case your numbers come up the following week!

I've been going along a bit later every night as the daylight hours have been getting longer – thieves and vandals don't tend to operate unless there's a cover of darkness. I was a bit late going up to the building this time because the last few nights have been icy cold in the churchyard despite it being the middle of summer, and having shivers running up your spine when you're on your own in a graveyard in the middle of the night is not something I would recommend!

I suppose I'd been trying to put off going up there altogether, but the church has got to have someone to look after it and apart from Alf and myself, and maybe Amelia, there was no one else who was going to do it, and the other two are a bit past it for wandering about looking for criminals in the darkness.

Anyway, I took my torch with me as usual and walked from my house on The Green up the High Street past the horse chestnut trees up to the churchyard. It was deathly quiet there – no breeze, no sound anywhere, either there or behind me in the village – and once again it was surprisingly cold. It was a cloudless night but there was no moon; the only light came from the dim yellowness of the streetlamps in the High Street behind me. It was very dark everywhere else. I pulled my collar up around my neck, swallowed hard and opened the gate.

I walked along the main path, on the gravel as usual, trying to tread as heavily as I could to alert any potential vandal to my presence, but still I could barely hear my footsteps over the beating of my heart.

I shone my torch around from left to right in front of me as I walked, and I had just about reached the building when the battery packed up. I suppose I had been using the torch a lot lately and the beam had been getting weaker, but it gave up the ghost rather suddenly and I was temporarily lost as to what to do.

I looked to my left towards the rectory, a hundred yards away, but there were no lights on. Alf had presumably retired to bed. I had to envy him at that moment, I must say! Here I was in the middle of the churchyard at night, in complete darkness, surrounded by complete silence and possibly with a gang of thieves or vandals hidden somewhere around waiting to jump out on me. What on earth should I do?

Having stood still for a few moments in contemplation, listening to my heart beating loudly in my ears, I decided that as I was there and I would have to walk back to the High

Street in darkness anyway, I might as well make a circuit of the church as usual, and be done with it. So I carried on up the path, stamping louder than ever on the gravel to alert anyone who was hiding there to my presence.

I reached the porch and peered into the darkness of the main doorway. My eyes had not quite adjusted to the dark yet and I found it difficult to make anything out. I had stopped walking by now, and the pounding of my heart seemed to reverberate around the still and quiet graveyard with the force of a blacksmith's hammer on an anvil. Was that something moving on the floor in the darkness? I swallowed hard and leaned forward to get a closer look.

Suddenly, a dog barked in the distance down the hill by the crossroads, and I stood bolt upright as the sound went through me. At that same instant I saw a pair of eyes glowing in the darkness low down in the porch, and I let out a gasp of fright.

"Aah!"

Responding to this sudden noise, the rector's cat ran out of the porch, through my legs and off towards the rectory. My throat went dry, my heart missed several beats, and I held onto the porch wall for support.

When I had calmed down I allowed myself a smile. Some man I was! A cat would hardly be burgling or vandalising the church. Only mankind was capable of a crime like that. Fancy being scared of an animal!

It took me a few minutes to regain my composure and I stood still by the porch for a little while, letting my eyes become accustomed to the darkness, and listening to the dog barking sporadically in the distance. I felt more comfortable now, but I still couldn't help feeling that there was something amiss, almost like I was being watched by somebody.

I looked up at the church roof to check on my repairs to the slates but there was nothing moving there and it was too dark to see them properly anyway.

I decided to continue my walk along the path on the south side of the church towards the top of Church Lane. This would, after all, be the most likely route by which any vandals would enter the churchyard, as it led in from the main road and yet was away from the village, so was not lit by streetlights like the High Street was.

I reached the gate at the top of Church Lane and peered down the road to see if there was any movement. The dog was still barking, but there was no sign of Man. A badger rustled in the shadows of the hedgerows. At least I think it was a badger – I've never actually seen one in the wild and I've joked with Alf before now that I don't think such a creature actually exists!

Anyway, all was quiet in the lane so I turned back into the churchyard and walked around the tower to the northern side of the church. The weak light coming from the High Street was temporarily blocked out by the church building – this was the darkest part of the entire churchyard.

There was no gravel path to stamp on around this side either, and the grass was quite long and difficult to walk in – mowing it was my next job! The barking was getting louder as the dog progressed from the crossroads up towards the church. I wasn't sure whose dog it was, but I guessed it must have sniffed out the badger or some other night-time creature. I rather welcomed the sound actually – I didn't feel quite so alone.

Not, that is, until something grabbed my leg...

At least I think it did. The long grass pulled on my feet with every step as I lifted them up to walk. I stood in one clump that sort of recoiled under my step and then wrapped around my leg. I tried to lift my foot but it held fast. I couldn't shake it off. I kicked out but the grass clump stuck to me. I kicked again harder. The dog barked closer and louder. I kicked again. Then there was a cry. A long, loud, piercing, shrieking cry, coming from Church Lane.

Something had happened to the dog.

I kicked my leg again. And again. I began to panic!

I kicked again and again and again.

There was a sound of scuffling in Church Lane.

I kicked again and again – and at last the clump of grass gave up its hold on me. It came up with my foot and was flung off into the darkness. There was a whimpering sound from the dog's direction and a hissing, muttering sound seemingly emanating from the clump of grass as it landed.

A violent spasm seized control of me and I let out a scream.

"Heeelp!"

But I could hardly get the word out, I was so choked up with fear.

So I did what anyone in trouble does next. I ran.

I ran and I ran and I ran. As fast as my legs could carry me. Past the church, past the gravestones, past the bushes. The grass couldn't hold me now. There was only one thing on my mind. Get to the light of the High Street. Now! Injured dog or no, I had time only for me at that terrifying moment. And there was not anywhere near enough of that as far as I was concerned!

I reached the churchyard gate and ran past the lock-up. Underneath the streetlights. Through the silent houses. Never daring to look back. Intent on getting home.

I got in a little while ago, slammed and locked the door behind me, and turned on all the lights and sank petrified into a chair, with my heart pounding throughout my body. I sat there for ages, too frightened to move. I am only just about now regaining my composure.

I never saw any vandals. And quite frankly I don't fancy ever going up there at night again to check for any. What on earth is going on in this village of late? Heaven only knows.

If I ever do have to go up there again I thank God this is the latest time of day I will have to do so. The night of the summer solstice. The day with the longest daylight hours. The nights will be drawing in again from now on. I never thought I'd welcome the news of that!

Cutting from the *Thamesmouth Evening Star*, Tuesday, 22nd June, pasted into Stephen Varley's journal and shown to Mr. Edward Glass, Chief Constable of South Anglia Police, on Tuesday, 28th September:

PET DOG KILLED BY HIT-AND-RUN DRIVER

The bloodstained body of a family's beloved pet dog was found this morning by a farmhand in Church Lane, Cannow's End.

Tess, whose owners live near the busy crossroads at the foot of the hill leading up to All Saints Church, is thought to have been the victim of a hit-and-run traffic accident.

The four-year-old black-and-white Border collie was let out into the garden just after midnight last night and ran barking into the darkness after an unknown animal, thought to be a cat. She failed to return home, and was found in Church Lane this morning with a deep gash in her left side, apparently caused by heavy impact with a speeding vehicle. The crossroads at the foot of the hill is known to be dangerous and Tess appears to have been the latest victim of speeding night-time traffic. Her family is said to be in deep shock.

Police are appealing for witnesses.

Extract from the minute book of the Parochial Church Council of All Saints Church, Cannow's End, meeting at Miss Cartwright's house, Wednesday, 21ˢᵗ July at 6.00 p.m.

4. *Pigeons in Church Tower*

Reverend Park reported that he had had several complaints from parishioners about the number of pigeons currently occupying the church tower. They were creating mess and noise which many local residents were finding unbearable. People didn't mind a few pigeons, he reported, but they felt that there were generally too many. Other members of the PCC had had similar feedback.

It was agreed that the PCC should investigate humane methods of pigeon control.

...

Cutting from the *Marnham Evening News*, Monday, 2nd August, pasted into Stephen Varley's journal and shown to Mr. Edward Glass, Chief Constable of South Anglia Police, on 28th September:

'RIPPER-STYLE' MURDER IN ALENORTH

Police are hunting a 'Ripper-style' murderer after the discovery of a mutilated woman's body in Marsh Lane, Alenorth. The secluded spot, on the north bank of the River Crouch opposite Cannow's End, is a romantic location and the frequent haunt of courting couples, and it is thought that the murderer may well have taken his victim there under the pretence of a passionate encounter.

Residents of the Marsh Farm caravan park – the only homes in the vicinity of the lane – said they heard screaming just after midnight, and several of them called the police. Mr. Stephen Samuels, whose caravan is closest to the end of Marsh Lane, went out onto the sea wall to investigate with a torch but was knocked over by a badger running past him which was evidently frightened by the screams. His torch fell into the river and the light promptly went out. He made his way back to his home and waited for the police to arrive.

Police have confirmed that they received several calls from members of the public at around 12.15 a.m. and sent two officers from Marnham to investigate. They have also confirmed that the badly mutilated body of a woman in her early thirties has been found in undergrowth on the east side of Marsh Lane, but they are not yet releasing her identity.

Precise details of the victim's injuries have not been released, but early reports suggest that her abdomen was slashed open with a knife.

Anyone who saw anything suspicious is asked to get in touch with police, who have set up a mobile incident room at the scene.

Extract from Stephen Varley's journal, Monday, 2nd August, shown to Mr. Edward Glass, Chief Constable of South Anglia Police, on Tuesday, 28th September:

6:50pm

I've just seen the local news on TV and there was a story on there about the horrific murder of a woman in Alenorth, just across the river from here. My blood ran cold as I watched it – it sounded horrible, like the Yorkshire Ripper murders of the late 1970s.

I have been concerned for some time that something strange is going on in Cannow's End, and now there is a horrible murder just across the water. I can't help feeling that there is some sort of connection and that this is just the latest and most horrific in a seemingly never-ending series of incidents to have occurred locally of late.

First, in February, we had those freak weather conditions. Then, in May, the church was vandalised. In June there was that terrifying 'dead dog' night and now there's a murder across the river in August. I've been cutting out items from newspapers and magazines and sticking them into my journal as they have happened, and looking back over them now I can feel the hairs standing up on my head.

Are all these things connected, or is it just this spooky village that is giving me the willies when there is a quite logical expla-nation for everything? I can't believe at the moment that it's all coincidence. I'm going to do a bit of research into Cannow's End history and see what I can come up with...

Extract from the coroner's report to Mr. Edward Glass, Chief Constable of South Anglia Police, Wednesday, 11th August:

Edward,

I have concluded my investigations into the cause of death of the female discovered in Marsh Lane, Alenorth on Monday, 2nd August and I intend to report to the authorities as follows…

The victim died of multiple stab wounds to the legs, face, abdomen and arms, many evidently incurred in trying to fight off the killer. The weapon used was a short, curved knife, probably only four inches long, but it was employed in a slashing fashion rather than 'in-and-out'. This caused much damage to the skin and internal organs of the victim. The whole escapade must have been horrifying for the poor girl, but at least death would have occurred pretty quickly.

Traces of blood and saliva which do not belong to the victim have been found on the body, and we are currently running tests in conjunction with your officers in an attempt to find a match with known or suspected murderers in other cases.

The inquest will be held on Friday, but I thought you would appreciate an early indication of my findings.

Jerry Patterson, Coroner

**Photocopy of an article from *Mysterious Essex Places*
magazine (back issue, volume 2, number 6,
found in Thamesmouth Library), sellotaped into
Stephen Varley's journal and shown to Mr. Edward
Glass, Chief Constable of South Anglia Police,
on Tuesday, 28th September:**

THE REPORTED HISTORY OF

CANNOW'S END AND ITS CHURCH

Much has been written about the village of Cannow's End
in south-east Essex and its supposed supernatural associa-
tions. Amongst other things, the place has an unenviable
reputation for witchcraft, having some of the strongest
connections with the so-called 'black arts' in the whole
country. Even as recently as the 1890s there were recorded
sightings of diabolical occurrences and happenings, and
tradition still persists to this day that there are witches
actively practising in the village even now.

Eric Sycamore's authoritative *Witchcraft World* (Halt
Press Ltd, 1962), devotes a whole section to Cannow's End
and its witchcraft tradition, claiming that there is nowhere
else in the British Isles where the belief in witchcraft
persisted so long and so intensely, and where legends of
old dark magic were told only a generation ago by the
fireside to scare little children. Little wonder, he says,
that this settlement has always been known – and still is
known – as 'The Witching Village'.

Sycamore found that visitors to this remote area in the early 19th century declared the whole population, from lord of the manor to the humblest peasant, to be continually obsessed by the fear of the unknown. The tradition of witchcraft overhung the whole village like a shadow of death.

Other research has focused on particular individuals in the village who were known to have been possessed with magical powers. One of the most significant of these was the legendary 'cunning man' or wizard, George Gill. Gill certainly looked the part – one researcher has written that he was tall, gaunt and looked very forbidding. A single glance from his cold blue eyes sent shivers down the spines of villagers and visitors alike. Gill had, amongst other things, the apparent ability to influence the workings of farm machinery and owned several 'familiars' – spirit-beings which were like pets – which he could command to make mischief whenever and wherever, and on whomever, it suited him to do so. He was also thought to be in league with the legendary 'nine witches of Cannow's End', and his power over them was so great that he had only to stand on his doorstep and whistle, and they would all appear.

The village church of All Saints, perched high on the hill overlooking the River Crouch, is the centre of much of this tradition, and the wealth of legends and stories surrounding the building serves to underline and amplify the claims of Mr. Sycamore and other researchers.

There is a belief, for example, that a stone fell from the church tower every time one of the nine witches (referred to above) died. Another legend states that if a person circles the church alone at midnight, the witches and ghosts of the village will come out and sing to him or her, whilst ghostly bells can sometimes be heard ringing in the river down below.

Jessica Paynter, in her book *Essex Ghosts* (Jonathan David Publications, 1987), reports that the Essex Paranormal Research League, a psychic group set up to investigate paranormal events in the county, visited All Saints in 1957 and recorded several unusual experiences there, including a strange atmosphere in the oldest part of the church, a strange psychic coldness near the altar, and a weird light around the top of the tower.

The churchyard itself is reputed to be haunted by the ghost of a headless woman, probably a witch and usually dressed in silk, who has been seen riding on a hurdle (a type of fence) down the hill from the church to the river, where she mysteriously disappears into thin air. Another female ghost, said to rise up from one of the tombstones in the churchyard, has also been seen.

Even the nearby rectory does not escape a supernatural association. The *Thamesmouth Evening Star* reported in 1963 that the ghost of a young girl had been seen in the driveway and that doors in the building often seemed to open and shut of their own accord.

In recent years, the church has become something of a Mecca for witch hunters on the important October festival of All Hallow's Eve or Halloween (31st). Hundreds of (mainly young) people from all over Essex – and probably from further afield, too – converge on the church each year to witness... well, it is not really clear what they expect to witness, though presumably, on this special night, it would be some sort of phenomena to support the traditions identified by some of the stories indicated above.

Perhaps one of the most fascinating legends is that if one runs three times anticlockwise round the church at midnight on Halloween it is possible to go back in time! Maybe some of these youngsters are trying to attempt that?

Whatever their particular reasons for being there, one curious side effect of the witch hunters' attentions is undeniable. A huge police presence, perhaps as many as a hundred officers, is employed to block off all accesses to the church from early evening onwards every October 31st. None but Cannow's End residents are allowed within several hundred yards of the building until well into the early hours of the following morning, by which time even the most determined of witch hunters has usually been defeated by the autumn cold. Understandably, Cannow's End residents do not take kindly to this annual event of shouting, car door slamming and, because of the season, firework explosions, but the intriguing question remains: why bother to prevent everyone from approaching the building if there really is nothing happening there? Surely if everyone was allowed to visit All Saints one year and prove to themselves that there was nothing unusual taking place, and thus nothing worth going there for in subsequent years, all curiosity would be satisfied and no one would be in the least bit concerned about visiting the place on future Halloweens. The enormous waste of police manpower would be freed to catch real criminals, and residents of the village would be left in peace once and for all.

Why indeed?! To many people, this continued ban on visiting a place of worship on a night of special significance merely emphasises the fact that there must be something there worth seeing. Many would dearly love to find out why the church is the subject of so much attention on Halloween.

Photocopy of an article taken from a book entitled *Everything You Wanted To Know About Druids, But Were Afraid To Ask*, borrowed from Thamesmouth Central Library, pasted into Stephen Varley's journal and shown to Mr. Edward Glass, Chief Constable of South Anglia Police, on Tuesday, 28th September:

Dates of special significance in the Druid calendar are as follows:

2nd February	Candlemass (Imbolc) – a time of natural beginnings, cleansing and planting
21st March	Spring Equinox (Alban Eiler) – seeds and wine, stimulus, blossom, magic
1st May	Beltane (Bealteinne) – the first day of summer, the good fire and pentagram, blossom, magic
21st June	Summer Solstice (Alban Heruin) – high point of light, clearing of sight
1st August	Lammas (Lughnasadh) – some harvest and sacrifice (main harvest is 23rd September), ripening
23rd September	Autumn Equinox (Alban Elued) – harvest, the garnering of the wisdom of Life, realisation of dark days ahead
31st October	Halloween (Samhuinn) – the dead returning to the living, the timeless ones, eternity
21st December	Winter Solstice (Alban Arthuan) – death and birth, renewal and healing

These dates are determined to honour the sun, moon and the earth and to provide a cyclical framework around which the ancients used to orient their lives. The role of women and goddesses is prominent in Druid religion, as are the roles of air, earth, fire and water and the building of stone circles.

Annotated note, handwritten on the photocopy by Stephen Varley and dated 17th August:

On all these dates from 2nd February to 1st August inclusive, something weird has happened in Cannow's End! If there's a strange occurrence on 23rd September there is definitely something afoot!

Extract from Stephen Varley's journal, Tuesday, 14th September, shown to Mr. Edward Glass, Chief Constable of South Anglia Police, on Tuesday, 28th September:

7pm

Alf died today, in the early hours of the morning, apparently from a heart attack. He was found lying on the rectory path that leads to the church. It's all very sad. I know he was getting a bit doddery, but he was still the only real friend that I had in the village apart from Amelia now, and he was probably the most respected person in it, too. I've written to my parents to give them the bad news.

Rumours have been circulating already about Alf's successor. He had been rector of this parish for so long that no one ever thought he was going to leave it, and his death did come about quite suddenly. There's talk that we'll be getting a female rector as a replacement – that should be a shock to the local 'status quo'. The death of the old order and the beginning of the new!

Extract from Stephen Varley's journal, Tuesday, 21st September, shown to Mr. Edward Glass, Chief Constable of South Anglia Police, on Tuesday, 28th September:

8pm

Alf was buried today. The whole village turned out to see him off. He was buried in his family's plot, apparently the last of the line.

My parents came to the funeral and were very upset. They came round here for tea afterwards and have only just left.

It's been quite a day all round, actually. I met the new rector today, Susannah Black. She wasn't terribly diplomatic, walking round the churchyard, inspecting the church building inside and out, even while the funeral service was going on. Reverend Peter Yexley from neighbouring Bashingham church took the service – Alf and he had been friends for ages.

I thought it a bit strange to say the least that Reverend Black should choose the time of a funeral service – and particularly that of her immediate predecessor – to wander round and look at her new church, but I overheard a couple of the older villagers talking about her and it seems as if she's from an old local family herself, though this is the first time she has ever been here. They didn't seem to have much time for her and she's not going to make herself terribly popular with anyone if she carries on like that!

I got to talk to her myself later on and I don't know if it's because she struck me as a busybody-type woman, but my first impression was that I wouldn't trust her further than I could throw her! She asked me lots of pointed questions about how the parish was run, what sort of things Alf did, what the church was like, whether people attended services, what did I think of the future of the Church, did it have a future, did women fit into that future? etc., etc. She certainly wasn't shy of asking difficult questions! Hardly the best way to make friends and influence people! I referred her to Amelia for answers to the questions I couldn't answer. She said she'd speak to her later "if I have the time"!

A new chapter in Cannow's End's history is obviously about to dawn.

Extract from Stephen Varley's journal, Thursday, 23rd September, shown to Mr. Edward Glass, Chief Constable of South Anglia Police, on Tuesday, 28th September:

6pm

I have spent the last few weeks studying Cannow's End and its past, and a terrible feeling of foreboding has been creeping over me with every word that I have read. The village has a long history of witchcraft, extending even to the present day. All the things that have happened over the past few months tie in with ancient Druid dates. I am dreadfully afraid for the future. And now Alf has gone I don't know who to turn to for support. Should I say something to Amelia? Or to my parents? And what on earth is going to happen next?

The death and funeral of Alf have not helped my demeanour – I feel really depressed and gloomy, even though I didn't know him that well – and his successor is doing her best to put everyone's noses out of joint. People seem to be a little intimidated by her or scared of her.

I can't help feeling from all I've read and seen that this village has been possessed by some recently reawakened power, and I have no idea what to do about it. If I go to the police they will denounce me as a madman, especially as I write fiction for a living. I'm too scared to talk to anyone else in the village in case they are a witch! I'm seriously thinking of moving again! Thank God I only decided to rent the house for a year and not buy it outright!

But then I think, "It's just your imagination. Calm down, think rationally and everything will be OK." But will it?

Tonight is the Autumn Equinox – one of the special dates in that supernatural calendar that I found. The air around the village seems electric – I don't think it's just me. I've tried not to talk to people today as my mind is in turmoil. I caught a glance from old Violet Egerton, and her eyes were red like they were on fire. I stared at her for several seconds before I realised what I was doing, and she just smiled a horrible smile at me and turned away. She's the one person I have seen Reverend Black getting on with.

Something is bound to happen tonight and I fear that the churchyard will once again be centre stage. Frightened though I am about the prospect, I know that I must go up there to collect more evidence. I am certain that something is going on, and perhaps after tonight I will be able to go to the police with something concrete. I'd rather not go up there on my own, but there isn't anyone else I can trust. I pray to God that I make it back in one piece.

Extract from Stephen Varley's journal,
Friday, 24th September, shown to Mr. Edward Glass,
Chief Constable of South Anglia Police,
on Tuesday, 28th September:

7:30 a.m.

Oh, my God! I have never seen anything quite so horrifying, quite so frightening, quite so incredible, as the scene I saw last night. I must write it all down while it's clear in my mind. I will convince myself later that I imagined it, if I don't write it down now.

After my experience in the churchyard in June, I was not looking forward to standing around in the dark again, with who knows what going on around me. I decided that the safest place to be would be inside the church building, the door of which I locked behind me and tested several times for security before I was satisfied. I checked all other doors and windows, and locked them. It's the first time the building's been locked at all in ages, but Amelia has given me the spare keys to look after now she's getting too frail to look after the building herself, and I decided that I was going to use them! The electricity wasn't working again for some reason – seemingly the control panel in the vestry that was repaired in May had developed a fault. I lit a candle and sat by the table, wondering what to do next and whether anything would happen.

I sat there for some time, reading through an old history book about all the church's former rectors, which I had found in the vestry, waiting for the time to tick slowly round to midnight, which I guessed would be the most likely hour if anything was going to happen.

Just before twelve I heard the wind getting up outside and whistling around the church building. Leaves were rustling in the churchyard. I put my book down and stood up. Suddenly there was a bang on the door as if something had blown against it and the door moved backwards and forwards sharply several times, as if someone was trying to open it. The flame on my candle flickered and blew out. I picked up the two torches I had brought with me (I was taking no chances after June's incident!) and shone one of them against the door. It seemed to be bowing inwards from pressure outside. The wind howled outside like an animal and the door rattled and rattled, as did the windows all around me.

Suddenly, behind me, there was a loud tapping on one of the nave windows on the north side and I spun around, startled. The curled branches of a tree, looking like animals' claws, were rapping the glass, making screeching, scratching sounds as they did so. The hairs on the back of my neck stood on end and a shiver ran up my spine. All around me the windows and doors were rattling and creaking – it was like all the full force of Nature herself was trying to get into the building, but there was something very unnatural about it.

In a panic, and scared of I don't know what, I looked around for somewhere to hide. The nearest safe place was the spiral stairway leading up to the tower, which had a door I could lock behind me. Carrying my keys and torches, I ran to the tower stairs, pulled the door open, and entered the narrow stairway. I pulled the door tight behind me and locked it. This was definitely the most secure place in the whole building, with thick stone walls built to keep out an army. The stairs spiralled upwards above me to the roof of the tower. The heavy lead hatch at the top, which provided access onto the tower roof, was, along with the vestry door at the north-east corner of the building, just about the only entrance that was always kept locked.

I panned my torch up the curving wall of the tower stairs enclosure and, in a brief moment of lucidity, pondered on how long it must have been since someone last went up to the top of the tower. We didn't usually open it all the way because we had no real need to go higher than the ringing chamber, and we had long since discontinued public open days once the insurance premiums had become too prohibitive. I certainly hadn't been up it, and Alf and Amelia probably hadn't been up there for years.

The position I was in was cocooned somewhat from the ferocious, howling winds which I could hear faintly all around me, and I sat down on the stairs for a while, wondering what to do next.

Suddenly, there was loud bang, like metal breaking, and a delayed thud – the sound of wood against stone. Was that the church door being broken open?! Surely the wind wasn't that strong!

A change in the air pressure inside the building rattled the locked door in front of me at the bottom of the stairwell. I jumped to my feet and looked about me. I was certainly secure here, but it suddenly dawned on me that I was also trapped: one end led to the nave, probably now open to the elements with the main church door having been blown open; the other led up to the top of the tower with nowhere to go but the roof. Neither option was particularly enticing.

A clattering sound in the nave decided me. I raced up the stone steps towards the ringing chamber – I could lock myself in there if necessary.

I reached the first narrow window slit in the tower, now blocked up with Perspex, and tried to peer outside. It was totally dark, so I rubbed the transparent material to clear off some of the dust and pressed my nose against it to peer out. As I did so, a face on the other side looked in at me, and I jumped back in fright. I shone my torch at the opening and it reflected back at me – there was nothing there. It must have been my own reflection! All this wind and noise and all this bad feeling I had been getting was playing tricks with my imagination and I laughed at myself, not least for the reassurance.

Then I became aware of something soft pressing against my hand.

I started again, jumped up, and turned my torch on the spot in question.

Pigeon feathers. That was all they were – pigeon feathers. We used to have loads of pigeons in this church, but their numbers had been declining rapidly over the past couple of months for some reason. Apparently something to do with the unseasonably cold August weather.

I played the torch across the feathers and saw that spots of dried blood lay on many of them. The shafts of some of them were broken in half. It looked as if the bird which had once owned them had been eaten by a cat – but a cat couldn't have got into the church tower...?

The door at the bottom of the stairwell rattled below me and I started again.

I shone the torch down the stairs but could not see the door around the curve of the inside wall. I shone the torch above me and saw the door to the ringing chamber, where the bellringers stood when they rang the church bells, and I headed for that as a haven of safety.

I spent ages in the ringing chamber, waiting for the wind to die down and for my heart to return to its normal beat. I could vaguely hear rattling in the nave, and the wind was still blowing around the outside of the building. It had even evidently also found its way through cracks into the bell chamber above me, for I could hear the bells clanking periodically with every strong gust, and the dangling bell ropes coming down from them were dancing all around me all the time like snakes from a snake-charmer's basket.

I shone my torch against the window of the ringing chamber and could see that it was slightly bowed as the wind blew against it, as if the wind was trying to push it in. The window itself was a bit too high up from the floor for me to look out of, so I just sat there in the darkness for ages, with my torch in my hand, switched off now but ready to be switched on again at a moment's notice, listening intently to everything going on around me.

Eventually things quietened down a bit outside and I plucked up the courage to venture out of the room. I turned my torch on and opened the door to the stairwell, looking alternately up and down, but there was nothing untoward in evidence.

I stepped into the stairwell and was preparing to go down when it occurred to me that it might be safer to establish the 'all clear' from the top of the tower, where I would have a good view of the whole of the surrounding churchyard, so I set off in that direction instead.

All the way up from the ringing chamber, past the bell chamber where the bells themselves were housed, right up to the top of the tower, there were bloodstained pigeon feathers like the ones I'd seen lower down. Perhaps a cat had got into the tower after all? Maybe I would come across the bones of that shortly too?!

I reached the top of the building and climbed up the wooden ladder, which rested on the top stone step, to unlock the lid which led out onto the top of the tower. I stood up with my shoulders pressed hard against the heavy lead panel, my feet braced on the ladder's rungs, and lifted it off out onto the roof. The cold night air came in unexpectedly and I drew a deep breath, but at least the wind had ceased.

I clambered up out onto the roof, crept over to the northern edge of the tower, and peered over the parapet into the darkness. I had to hold on to the stonework as I staggered back in horror at the scene that lay before me. The whole of the churchyard below me was alive.

There was just enough light from the yellow streetlamps in the High Street for me to be able see what was going on. There were four large, dog-like creatures, scavenging around in the graveyard like a pack of hungry wolves. Two of them had stopped to sniff and paw at the ground where Alf had been buried only a few days previously and they were whining excitedly, as if they had found something they were looking for, and growling in delight.

But these dog-like creatures were not dogs. I wasn't even sure they were mammals. The little illumination that there was from the yellow streetlights gave only the faintest glimpse of what they were as they prowled round in the shadows. They were animals of a kind I'd never seen before. One looked a bit like a monkey, and was another one a dragon??

I looked on in horror, squinting my eyes to try to make out more detail in the darkness.

Having been cooped up in the tower stairwell and ringing chamber for some time, much of it without light, I was becoming pretty much accustomed to the dark – though still not quickly enough for my liking at that moment.

They were digging now, these creatures, at dear old Alf's grave. Digging and digging like excited dogs uncovering a bone. They fought each other playfully but roughly as each took its turn to try to dig down. I choked my emotions back and stifled a cry. They were digging up Alf's grave!

I watched them as they dug, faster and faster, with greater excitement all the while. Clods of earth went sailing into the darkness. The noises they were making were getting louder too.

This was sacrilege! I could stand it no longer.

I stood up and switched on my torch and pointed it down at them.

"OI!" I shouted at the top of my voice, the words sticking in my throat. "LEAVE ALF ALONE!"

They stopped digging almost instantaneously, and turned in unison to look up at me.

"Leave Alf alone," I said a bit more quietly, taking a step backwards.

They stood breathing heavily from their exertion there like big dogs panting after a long run. Their tongues were hanging out, and for the first time, I could make out the whites of their eyes. They looked at each other and then back at me. I could feel that something horrible was about to happen.

"SHOO!" I shouted at them this time, clearing my throat to regain my full voice. "GO AWAY!"

They paid no attention. They simply seemed to sneer at me in a way that I'd only ever seen Man sneer before: a kind of supercilious, superior sneer as if to say "I am in charge and there's nothing you can do about it".

One of them – the monkey – rose on its haunches and looked at me with contempt. The others bared their teeth like ferocious dogs about to make an attack. I panned my torch over them, picking out features faintly in the darkness – teeth, claws, even wings! As my torch panned over their features I felt a wave of nausea come over me, clutched onto the tower stonework even more tightly for support, and had a horrible foreboding feeling that I was going to die.

I tried to shout "Leave me alone!", but it just came out as a whisper. My throat was dry and the words were stuck in my gullet.

The hideous beasts stood up straight now, some on four legs, some on two.

I felt behind me with my feet for the hatch.

One that looked like a bat let out a bloodcurdlingly hideous scream and took off in flight towards me.

I staggered backwards, ran to the hatch and jumped inside, grabbing at the heavy lead covering as I did do. As I pulled it round to manoeuvre it into place over my head to block the entrance, it caught on the lip of the opening and stuck fast. It wouldn't drop into place!

I pulled and pulled, twisted and turned it, trying to fit it into its hole. The weight was heavy on my arms, the sweat heavy on my brow. I heard the sound of flapping wings and caught sight of a large, winged creature, with talons and a long tail, appearing over the parapet. I shouted in panic and gave the lid one last twist to pull it into place.

This time it worked! The creature disappeared as the heavy lead lid closed over the opening.

I lost my footing and fell into the darkened stairwell below me.

~ x ~

I came round hours later, lying in the half-light on the stairs as the sun struggled to glimpse me through the narrow window slits in the curving stairwell wall.

I awoke with a start. I didn't remember anything after closing the tower roof hatch and losing my footing. I must have blacked out when I fell.

I looked up at the tower hatch above me, solid lead, strong as anything, for signs of entry. There weren't any. It had held!

I looked at my watch. 6:07 a.m.!

I stood up stiffly, feeling my leg and head where they both had evidently hit the hard stone stairs. I picked up my torches and keys and inched my way up the ladder towards the lead hatch. It was solid all right, but the lead was dented from above, as if something had been pounding on it from the outside.

I wiped my forehead and ran the palms of my hands down my jumper.

What should I do?

I realised that with daylight coming, there would soon be other people around. I had no desire to spend any more time in the church than necessary, and decided that the best course of action was to make my way down to the nave and get outside the building and out into civilisation as quickly as I possibly could.

I crept down the half-lit stairwell to the door from the tower into the nave and listened carefully. There was no sound.

I turned the key in the lock and listened again. All was definitely quiet.

I gradually pushed the door open away from me and peeped out over the top of it. Everything seemed normal.

I was relieved to see that the main door of the church had held out, despite the noises and the clamour that I had heard during the storm and my imagination-haunted fears that it had been broken. I thanked the door's 16th-century workmen for the good, strong job they had done with it as I turned the key in the latch, opened it and stepped out into the churchyard. There were scratch marks on the outside of the door and as I caught sight of them I felt sick to the pit of my stomach.

Outside in the churchyard, the sun was trying to get up, and the amount of light was growing all the time. I breathed a sigh of relief and drunk in the refreshing morning air. There was a tree branch on the path near the porch, and the churchyard seemed to be in slight disarray.

I kicked up my heels and sped quickly away through the east entrance of the churchyard into the High Street. I was back home within minutes and after a stiff drink of vodka from the cabinet (yes, I know it's early!) I sat down to write this entry in my journal.

Stephen Varley's journal, Tuesday, 28th September:

6:15pm

I met this morning with Edward Glass, Chief Constable of the South Anglia Police, who came to my house for the purpose, and I showed him the contents of this journal which related specifically to all the strange incidents that have been going on here of late.

To my great surprise and much relief, he did not seem to find what I was saying to be too preposterous and instead listened intently to what I had to say, and appeared to read with interest the items that I had gathered and recorded.

After a light lunch, we went to the police information room outside the lock-up in the afternoon, where he photocopied some extracts from my journal and gave them to Detective Chief Inspector Rogers to put with the police files. He has asked me not to say anything to anyone else about this case and has suggested that I spend a couple of days with my parents. He knows them well from many years back from his time as a sergeant in Borley – his home village in north Essex and the neighbouring parish to my home town of Sudbury, where I grew up. He was quite forceful about it, almost as if he was trying to get me out of the area.

I must say I would be glad myself to get out of Cannow's End for a while and go back home and see my parents. I'll give them a ring in a minute and see if I can arrange it.

Despite the reassuring discussion with Mr. Glass, I am still much troubled by the events of the other night. Those creatures were REAL! I was NOT imagining it! But how can they have been real? One was a dragon, one was a bat and one was a funny-looking monkey! Dogs, I would have believed, but monkeys...?!

I'll make my excuses to Amelia and go away for a few days. I'm sure if nothing else the break will do me good.

Stephen Varley's journal, written in Sudbury church, Sunday, 3rd October:

1pm

Another surprise! Different, but just as unexpected as those back home!

I had a long talk last night and a briefer one this morning with my parents about everything strange that has happened in Cannow's End. I tried to keep it to myself but couldn't, and they evidently knew that something was wrong and tried to coax it out of me, and in the end I had to tell them. And how glad I am I did!

There is much more to all those strange goings-on than meets the eye, and how amazed I was to find that my parents knew almost as much about it as I did, all the way up here in Sudbury! This journal has already proved useful to refer back to, so I shall write everything they told me down here and now, so as to have it down as a reference source of everything, and not miss anything out.

~ x ~

I knew Alf personally for only about nine months, though I had often heard my parents talking about him. Mum's family and his went back many years, but I had never really probed the origins of their relationship before. I did so last night, with surprising results!

Mum's mum, who I never knew, had herself grown up in

Cannow's End and had known Alf when the two were in their childhood. They used to hang about together, swimming in the Crouch, playing conkers in the churchyard, and telling each other stories about Cannow's End's secret past.

Alf's mother was a member of the Gill family and was related to George Gill, the 'cunning man' I had read about in that book in Thamesmouth library. There was some talk that she was one of the witches that he controlled, but this was never proven. Alf's father had died when he was young and Alf had been brought up by his mother, under the guidance of George Gill, and was schooled for a career as a clergyman for the local community even from an early age.

Grandmother told Mum that when she and Alf were about seven or eight, George Gill, then an old man in his 90s, got into an argument with a middle-aged woman in the village, who seemed to be criticising him for meddling in her affairs. They had a big argument out in the street, shouting things at each other in some sort of foreign language. The woman was accusing him of breaking her cousin's farm machinery and riddling her yard with mice. Everyone else disappeared into their houses and only Grandmother and Alf – two young kids – were left on the street to see what was going on. They hid behind a cart to watch the argument.

The woman, Sarah Morton, known locally as the 'River Witch' from her connections with an Alenorth witchcraft family, made as if to strike George Gill but didn't actually touch him. The old man stumbled backwards and fell to the ground. Incensed, Grandmother came out from behind the cart and shouted at her to stop. The witch turned towards them and glared such a horrible glare that the two cowered behind the cart again and didn't dare move or say another word. After a few moments spent re-gaining his composure, Alf grabbed Grandmother's arm and took her off to get his mother, whom he knew would come to the aid of the stricken Gill. As they ran they could hear the two shouting at each other – Gill from the floor, the River Witch towering over him. Curtains in the cottages in the main street twitched as the argument raged.

When Grandmother and Alf returned with his mother, they found the River Witch gone and George Gill lying prostrate on the ground. He whispered something to Alf's mother about time coming to an end, and she picked him up off the ground and led him up the street into her cottage.

That night there was a terrible thunderstorm. The whole village seemed to be alive with noise and light. There was an oppressive humidity in the air and there were horrible wailing sounds emanating from the churchyard. It seemed to last for ever, the wind howling around Grandmother's cottage and branches of trees clattering against the weatherboarded buildings. On and on it raged, and Grandmother cowered ever deeper under the covers to try to hide from the wind and rain.

By morning the storm had died down and Grandmother got up early and went straight round to Alf's to compare notes of the event with him. When she arrived at his cottage she found a lot of the old women from the village already there, and there was a horse and cart with a black cloth laid out in the back of it outside the house. Pushing past the long, hanging dresses of the old women, Grandmother went into the main room and found Alf looking wistfully out of the window as if lost in thought. He smiled a bit when he saw her and the two of them left silently, leaving the women to crowd into one of the other rooms.

They walked up the main street in the direction of the church.

"Mr. Gill is dead," Alf told her, when they had got far enough away from the cottage to talk without being heard. "He died last night during the storm."

Grandmother didn't know what to say.

"Mother is very upset about it," Alf continued. "She keeps saying something about the ushering in of a different order and that Mr. Gill was too old and frail to resist it. I wish I knew what she meant."

The two of them walked in silence to the churchyard and sat on the gate by the lock-up, looking back down the main street. Neither of them knew what to say next, so they didn't say anything.

As they sat there, lost in their thoughts, preparations were being made in Alf's mother's cottage for the interment of George Gill. It did indeed feel like an old era had died, and with it something in them felt like it had died too.

- x -

They were awakened from their thoughts by a shrill, piercing voice immediately behind them.

"Never you mind about worrying, children," the voice's owner leered at them, and they jumped off the gate and looked round with a start.

Sarah Morton, the River Witch, was looking at them with a wicked grin. She leaned over the gate and pressed her face really close to theirs so that they could smell her horrible breath, and they recoiled in disgust. Her long black hair drooped over the gate and a black cat with deep green eyes rubbed up against her legs, peering at the children through the wooden bars.

"I'm in charge now," she said. Then she laughed a horrible laugh.

They didn't wait to hear any more. They turned on their heels and ran off down the street.

- x -

Neither Grandmother nor Alf ever forgot that day, but it had different effects upon them. Grandmother decided that she wanted to leave the village as the experience of the River Witch and the death of George Gill had frightened the life out of her and she didn't want to hang around in case such a thing ever happened again. As soon as she was old enough she went into service, taking a job in Sudbury, 40 miles from Cannow's End, and settled down to a life of peace and quiet. My mother was brought up in Sudbury, knowing little of the history of Cannow's End, all those miles away. Grandmother stayed in touch with Alf, her childhood friend, and he kept her informed about events in their home village. In due course, Grandmother died, Mum married Dad, and the stories of George Gill and the River Witch were forgotten.

Alf, on the other hand, had been stunned by the death of George Gill and the evident sadness it had caused his mother, and he vowed that he would stay around to protect her when she got old, and not let the River Witch hurt her again. Learning, as he grew older, that the foreign language that Gill and the River Witch had been shouting at each other was actually the language of witchcraft, he began to study witchcraft for himself and learned all the signs and symbols and chants of that art. He had inherited some of George Gill's abilities and soon found that he could cast small spells such as whistling up the wind when the day was otherwise calm, or getting fish to swim into his nets in the River Crouch. He apparently had several crises of conscience, trying to reconcile this with his service to God, but I guess he ultimately felt that God needed him to do it.

As he grew in age and strength an uneasy tension grew up over the village. The River Witch, who had been in charge since George Gill's death, was herself growing older and as age took its toll she also became weaker, just like Gill had done before her. Alf qualified as a clergyman and secured his first posting at All Saints aged just 26 when the then incumbent, Roboshobery Morton, 63-year-old brother of Sarah, died suddenly one night a few days before Christmas.

The following Christmas Sarah Morton herself died, and a calmness came over the village such as had not been known for many years.

Only one thing troubled Alf about the passing of the River Witch. Two months before her death he had found her up at the church in another blinding thunderstorm, chanting and shouting at the church building as if trying to make it come to life. The first rustlings of the leaves around the rectory had alerted him to the fact that something was amiss, and he went out into the High Street to spy on the River Witch's cottage and see if she was up to anything. When he arrived there, she was obviously absent – all he could see through the window was a baby girl, about two years old, left alone, asleep in her cot. He had no idea whose child this was.

With the wind picking up all the time, he struggled his way back up the High Street to the churchyard, fighting off branches and horse chestnut cases as they rained down on him from the trees near the east gate.

As he reached the gate, a fork of lightning flashed above him and he saw, silhouetted in the churchyard, the figure of Sarah Morton chanting incantations at the tower from her position by the north-east corner of the chancel. As she shouted, invoking some sort of spell, the wind and the lightning whipped up even more all around her, almost as if she was controlling it.

Alf knew that whatever she was doing, she was up to no good. He had to stop her.

"WITCH!" he shouted, and she looked across at him, startled, like a criminal caught by security guards just as he is about to break the code of a bank vault.

The church clock mechanism sounded the Westminster chimes – a common feature in public clocks, used to mark the quarter, half and three quarters of an hour, plus a prelude on the hour to the bells striking – and Alf himself jumped with a start. Was there some significance about the hour? The River Witch herself seemed alerted by the chiming and returned to her chanting, turning her back to Alf in defiance.

As the bells began to strike the hour Alf began subconsciously to count them as they went.

"One. Two…"

The River Witch continued her chanting, louder and faster, redoubling her efforts, as if to finish her spell.

"Witch!" Alf shouted again from the churchyard gate, bending forward with his arm across his face to fight off the wind that was howling round the eastern end of the church towards him and checking his progress.

"…Three…"

Still Sarah Morton cast her spells.

"...Four..."

With branches and leaves flying all about him, Alf considered what to do.

Stepping back a couple of paces, he took out his keys to the old village lock-up and opened first the strong outer iron gate and then the equally strong inner wooden door, which hid the darkness inside. He would try to get the witch into there.

"...Five... Six..."

Sarah Morton was still shouting, looking anxiously across now to see what Alf was doing.

"...Seven..."

Summoning up extra effort and shouting spells himself into the wind, Alf left the lock-up and pressed on into the churchyard, advancing ever nearer to the River Witch. The wind and lightning increased in intensity and they shouted against each other, louder and louder, like opera singers in the final act of a powerful tragedy.

"...Eight... Nine..."

Alf pressed on, closing in on the immobile River Witch all the time as she stood, stock still, legs apart, arms raised, invoking some evil power to do something to the church. He heard her words, but it was not a spell he knew. Nor had he time to understand it now.

"...Ten..."

As Alf closed in on the River Witch, she began visibly to weaken at the knees. As age took its toll, her power was decreasing and his was growing. He shouted directly at her now, counteracting the spell that she was trying to put in place. He pressed on against the wind, closing all the time.

"...Eleven..."

Finally, within reach of her, he summoned up the hidden reserves of strength that are always latent in young men, and jumped towards her, knocking her off her feet and pinning the evil old hag to the ground. There was a fearful scream from the other end of the churchyard, as if a wild animal had been caught in a trap, and a huge clap of thunder sounded overhead. Lightning illuminated the churchyard and Alf for the first time became aware of animals moving in the shadows, fleeing from the scene as he held the witch to the ground.

"...Twelve!"

Everything went quiet. The bells finished chiming, the thunder and lightning stopped, and the wind began to die down. The animals in the churchyard disappeared into the darkness and the River Witch went limp in Alf's grasp. She had hit the ground before twelve had sounded, but had he stopped her before she could finish her spell?

After a brief moment of rest, in which he began to regain his strength, Alf picked up the body of the River Witch, limp now with all her strength gone, and dragged her across the churchyard to the east gate. He lifted her up by putting his hands under her armpits, and carried her through the gate into the street. Outside the lock-up he held her against the opening, pausing as if thinking what to do, before casting the rag-doll body into the darkness and closing and locking the solid wooden door and iron gate behind her.

He was aware, as he trudged back to the rectory through fallen leaves and branches, of curtains twitching in the nearest cottages in the street. He was aware too, as he grappled to understand more of what the River Witch had been doing, about the significance of the date.

It was midnight on the 31st October. The time when Evil was at its strongest. All Hallow's Eve, or Halloween.

~ x ~

When dawn came on 1st November, Alf returned to the lock-up to let the River Witch out. She looked older and frailer and very, very ill. He took her to her cottage, unobserved by the villagers, and left her there with the young baby, which was still asleep. She began to regain some of her colour and he decided she would be OK, so he went back to the church.

The sun, rising in the east, picked out certain shadows on the building as Alf walked back towards it up the High Street. The two gargoyles on the east end really stood out in the light and for a fleeting moment Alf thought they were moving. He went inside the church and then did a circuit round the outside of it. The other two gargoyles at the west end of the building were also picked out from behind by the shadows of the sunrise more than he was used to. Everything appeared OK though, and he left the church with a warm feeling that the River Witch and her spells were at an end.

Sarah Morton never recovered fully from the Halloween incident, and died two months later at Christmas at the age of 65. The baby girl, apparently her granddaughter (although no one seemed to know she had a child of her own, let alone a granddaughter), was given to the care of another woman in the village – a friend of the River Witch who had grown up with her. Though they had not witnessed the incident, she and others in the village knew that something had happened that October, and that the balance of power had switched back from the Mortons to the Gills.

With the death of the River Witch a new calmness settled over the village. Alf, as rector and a revered relative of old George Gill, unspokenly held everything in balance. After a period of trauma, there was now at last a period of calm.

Extract from a book about pagan festivals, loaned to Stephen Varley by his parents and read by him in Sudbury church; also read by Michael Swain on, coincidentally, the very same day from a borrowed library book:

The modern festival of Halloween (31st October) derives from the ancient Celtic festival of Samhain (pronounced 'sa-ween'). It marks the beginning of the Celtic New Year and was seen by Celtic people as the one time of the year when the barriers between the living and the dead were removed. The dead were able to come back to the living world and pass on secrets and magical spells. It was traditional in some parts to dress up in costume as a way of protection by confusing the dead into believing that the people they encountered were not living beings but spirits. Candles were also lit to guide the way for the dead to return to their families.

The Celtic festival was later adopted by the Christian tradition and in some countries, such as in Latin America, it takes on a formal structure, with families visiting the graves of the departed, lighting candles and singing songs to them. Some parts of northwest England also maintain formal ceremonies, including the use of a 'night-mare' – a horse to carry away the dead on its back.

Over the years the darker elements of Halloween have come more to the fore, and there is a general feeling that there is something magical – but scary – about the evening of 31st October, culminating at midnight, which is seen by some as a time for human sacrifice, and there is also a fear that people will be attacked by the dead and or recruited into witchcraft against their will.

Black cats, broomsticks, pointed black hats, cauldrons, skeletons, masks, pumpkins with candles in them, trick-or-treating and even fireworks are all part of the modern Halloween tradition, but there is also a strong belief that Evil, especially regarding waking the dead, is predominant every 31st October.

Extract from the blog of Michael Swain, posted on the Internet on Sunday, 3rd October at 1.30 p.m.

i read that book abowt canowsend church and it sed the village had a history of superstishun an witchcraft, especially at halloween when loads of people go there! i also read a book abowt pagan festivals in general an it sed that lots of spooky peeple celebrate old-tyme superstishuns an stuff 2 all over the place at certain times of the year! omg! i also red an article in an old magazine called 'misterious essex places' or sumfink and it said in there that if u run rownd canowsend church anticlokwise three times at midnite on halloween u can go bak in time!

i begged keith cud we go to canowsend on halloween 2 c wot goes on 4 ourselves an run rownd the church an he woz like that sownds like a larf but we can only do it if u can learn how not to make any noise! lol! im reeding abowt detectives creepin abowt in me old man's novels 2 learn how 2b quiet, so i'll jus copy them.

im really getting excited abowt it now!

Stephen Varley's journal, written in Sudbury church, Sunday, 3rd October (continued):

I can't believe there's such a background to all this in Cannow's End! Why haven't my parents told me about it before? Why didn't Alf say anything? Maybe he just wanted to forget about it all! And to think my grandmother was involved as well!

All those creatures I saw the other night were obviously connected with all this witchcraft activity. The passing of Alf must have unleashed some new dreadful force that has taken over from him. But I thought all that witchcraft stuff was dead. Or was it just dormant?

So many questions!

I need to go back to Cannow's End to find out what's going on there now. Something even worse might have happened while I was away!

I'll give my leave to my parents. I'm sure they'll understand. I'll stay another night and then go back there tomorrow.

Story in the *Thamesmouth Evening Star*,
Monday, 4ᵗʰ October:

MAN ARRESTED IN 'SEVERED HEAD' CASE

The story of the severed head in Cannow's End church-yard ended with something of a whimper this morning when the police issued a statement saying that they had arrested a man for digging up Reverend Park's grave on the night of 23ʳᵈ September.

Questioning from our reporter on the scene at the mobile incident room in Cannow's End High Street led to further information being announced, and it seems that the man who has been arrested had a bit of an ongoing feud with Reverend Park and evidently felt that digging up his grave was a way of getting back at him. Police have described the man, reported as being from Alenorth, as "mentally unstable", which appears to be the cause of his bizarre behaviour.

The streets of Cannow's End were noticeably quieter today as Cannow's End people came to terms with the incident. Very little seems to be known about the alleged perpetrator of the crime, who is evidently not a Cannow's End resident. Older folk said that they remembered an old feud between their rector and an Alenorth man (some said a Cannow's End woman!), but they thought that had died down ages ago.

Operations at the incident room in the High Street seem to be being scaled down and there is, thankfully, an air of normality returning to the place.

The new rector, Reverend Susannah Black, said she was surprised at the speed with which the police had reached their conclusions, but was pleased that village life would be able to return to what it was before. As the new incumbent, she felt she had many challenges ahead of her and was looking forward to the task immensely.

The Chief Constable of South Anglia Police, Edward Glass, said he was pleased that investigations had turned up such a positive result so quickly, and that he hoped the media would now show less of an interest in the case.

The next step would seem to be the commission to trial of the unnamed arrestee. If anything else develops, you can be sure *Evening Star* reporters will be there to cover it for you.

Note pushed through Stephen Varley's door on the afternoon of Monday, 4ᵗʰ October:

Dear Mr. Varley,

Please get in touch with me as soon as you return.

I would like to discuss some issues with you.

Chief Constable Edward Glass, Cannow's End Incident Room

Stephen Varley's journal, Tuesday, 5th October:

12 noon

I returned home yesterday afternoon to find the newspapers playing down the story of the desecration of Alf's grave, and a note pushed through my door from Chief Constable Edward Glass.

I met with Mr. Glass this morning and discovered an even more amazing thing!

As with Alf, I knew Mr. Glass knew my parents, but I didn't know how well! He tells me now that he used to go out with my mother when he was living in Sudbury, and they met in the Red Lion's Head pub in Longchurch Road! Not only that, but he is as aware as they were about all the witchcraft stuff that has been going on here! Am I the only one who's been kept in the dark?

As I asked him more questions, another piece of the story began to come to light...

Alf had met my parents at my grandmother's funeral and become friends with them. Over a period of time he had told them about the various witchcraft activities. As teenage sweethearts, Mum and Mr. Glass had been 'soul mates' and Mum had shared with him her knowledge of Cannow's End's past. Alf, Mum and Mr. Glass had been reminiscing about this last year, and even more so this year once Alf had started telling Mum and Mr. Glass about all the strange things that had been happening. Mum phoned Mr. Glass on Sunday while I was in Sudbury church to tell him what she had told me about Alf and my grandmother. He consequently already knew some of the background when he came to the Incident Room in the High Street last weekend.

He also had a good grasp of Cannow's End traditions and had been reading up on them over the last week, just as I had been doing. He was from an old witchcraft family himself because Borley, too, it transpires, has a history of witchcraft and the supernatural, and he has had a lot of information about rites and practices passed down to him! The old rectory in Borley was famously haunted and when it was investigated at length by the well-known ghost-hunter, Harry Price, one of Mr. Glass's relatives is said to have gone along as an adviser.

He said he believed everything I had written in my journal, which was very reassuring, and would offer any help he could to finally put the matter to rest. When I asked him what he meant by that he said that Alf, representing Good, had died and that someone else, representing Evil, was obviously poised to take over and maybe had even contributed to Alf's death (much in the way that Mum told me Alf had done with the River Witch). Somebody, he said, needed to combat the Evil and restore the Good, and he was "pretty confident" that I was the right man! How he came to that conclusion, he never really explained!

I asked him about the investigations into the desecration of Alf's grave and he said that it was important to shut the newspapers up and not let the matter get out of hand. I asked him if he'd made the 'Alenorth feud' story up just to pacify the media. There was a twinkle in his eye as he flatly denied it to me!

I left with a piece of paper he had given me with a magazine title and page number on it – Historic Essex & Suffolk magazine, Spring 1912 (p.25) – and the need for another trip to Thamesmouth Library. He said he'd answer any more questions I had after I'd read that…!

Photocopy extract from *Historic Essex & Suffolk* magazine (Spring 1912) of an article entitled 'The History and Meaning of Gargoyles', sellotaped into Stephen Varley's journal Wednesday, 6th October:

One of the first sights that greets the traveller on his first arrival at the church of All Saints in Cannow's End is the hideous gargoyles on the nave and chancel. The ugly stone creatures have been deliberately positioned by some craftsman in the distant past to overlook both approaches to the churchyard, as if to keep a look out for someone and warning him to keep away.

The two at the western end – a dragon and a bat – seemed poised as if to fly out over the hill and down towards the marshes and the lowland area between here and Bashingham, like owls swooping over the fields for their prey. The two at the eastern end look equally as menacing – one in the form of a monkey, the other with a seemingly human face but hideously deformed. These look out over the High Street, the human community, as if watching that.

The origin of gargoyles goes back many centuries. Grotesque beasts were originally carved on the walls and under the eaves of churches to act as water spouts, though some have even been found on the buildings of Ancient Greece. Their name seems to derive from that of a legendary dragon known as 'Gargouille' that terrorised Rouen in France in the 7th century AD, but was killed by the Archbishop St Romanus. The word 'gargouille' means 'throat' or 'pipe'.

As time went on these grotesquely carved animal and human figures became more elaborate, reaching a peak in medieval times, when they appeared on many great cathedrals and churches throughout Europe. Devils, dragons, lions, monkeys, creatures in human form with tongues hanging out or rolling eyes and weird half-man/half-beast concoctions, some with several heads, all appeared during this period, instilling fear into everyone who caught sight of them.

The cathedral or church was central to the medieval way of life, and everyone attended to worship God. For those who could not read, fantastical pictures were used – wall paintings of these survive in many Essex churches. Many gargoyles were used in a similar way, illustrating Bible stories and retelling fables. The use of hideous and frightening creatures was a symbol to the population not to stray away from the path to Heaven as beasts of all kinds were lying in wait for them and would devour them and take them to the Devil in Hell. Eternal damnation for the wayward or the sinner was symbolised by these scary monsters in stone.

As time went on creatures became more and more grotesque, and many of them were sited at significant points of the building which they adorned to scare away evil spirits. Sexually explicit imagery was also used for this purpose. Figures of mixed gender or mixed species also occurred – beasts with human faces or humans with cloven feet. Heads too began to proliferate, providing a physical link back to the pagan days of headhunting Celts. Many of the figures took on threatening poses, serving to remind us that mankind is relatively insignificant and that there are greater forces at work around us than we can understand or control.

Note pushed through Stephen Varley's door on the morning of Wednesday, 6th October, while he was at Thamesmouth Library:

Stephen,

I called to discuss some important things with you. Please can you come and see me this afternoon, dear. There is much I need to discuss with you.

Thank you.

Amelia Cartwright

Stephen Varley's journal, Wednesday, 6th October:

8pm

I don't believe it! Are there any more secrets anyone wants to tell me?!

I got back from the library only to find a note from Miss Cartwright pushed through my door. She seemed to want to see me quite urgently so I went round to see her straight after lunch.

She was acting a bit strangely when I got there, almost as if she was desperate to tell me something but wasn't quite sure how I would react. Now I know why!

She began by saying that she'd had a phone call from my mother, of all people, telling her that I'd been up to Sudbury for a visit and that whilst I was there we had discussed Cannow's End's witchcraft history and the role of Alf and my grandmother in restoring the balance of Good versus Evil. She also said that she knew that Mr. Glass had been to see me and, putting two and two together with the newspaper report, had guessed that he was hushing things up and was looking to me for assistance.

I asked her if she was spying on me and she seemed a bit taken aback.

We talked for a while about the witchcraft implications and I was surprised that she too seemed to know a lot about it. She knew about George Gill, the River Witch and Mum's teenage liaisons with Mr. Glass. Did everyone know more about this than me? I began to get annoyed and jumped up and stamped around her old wooden cottage so hard that the beams above me seemed to creak and move.

Then she told me that my grandmother had been born Eileen Cartwright and Amelia was her younger sister, making Amelia my great-aunt!

I had never known my grandmother. She died at the young age of 45 when my mum was just 21 and I was not yet born. My mum's maiden name was Carter and by extrapolation her mum's married name would have been Carter too. I never thought to ask her maiden name! Amelia had been in bed ill when Eileen and Alf had witnessed the Gill-Morton argument, but her sister had told her about it and she had learned more from Alf later on as well. She hadn't said anything to me about it before because I was new to the village — and to her — and it wasn't the sort of thing you told strangers, but now she knew Mr. Glass had spoken to me she wanted to fill me in with what she knew as well. The final piece of the jigsaw that she slotted in very deftly, making as little outward fuss about it as possible, was to announce that her and Eileen's mother had been born Susan Gill, and that, like Alf, Susan was also related to George. Susan had therefore also inherited some of George's witchcraft powers, and these had descended through her into Eileen, Amelia, mother and ultimately me!

After I picked my jaw back up off the floor, I said a hasty 'goodbye' and went home to draw up my family tree — it all seemed so incestuous that I felt a pictorial representation was the only way to work it all out!

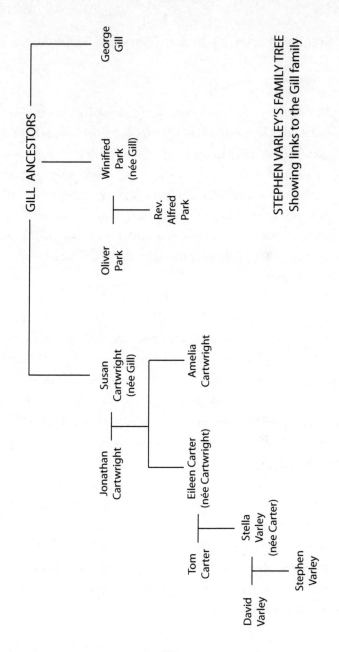

STEPHEN VARLEY'S FAMILY TREE
Showing links to the Gill family

Stephen Varley's journal, Thursday, 7th October:

11 a.m.

Well, I drew up the family tree and I've pasted it here in my journal, but there was so much information swirling around in my head about it that I couldn't relax, and as a consequence I didn't sleep very well at all. I dreamt all night about witches and I rose early after a restless sleep and went out for a walk to clear my head. I felt that I wanted to get away from this peculiar village and all its secrets. Away from the church and the rectory. Away from the cottage at the end of the lane where my great-aunt lives.

I turned east at the High Street and headed towards the King's Head pub, then left opposite that into Crouch Lane and down to the river. It was cold and there was a chilly breeze, but I had my coat buttoned tightly around me and it was warm inside it as I walked. One or two stars still sparkled in the sky and the moon picked up ripples in the Crouch as I made my way downhill across the cornfields, my head spinning with all the news that I had heard. Dawn was coming but the sky was still black rather than blue.

Past the old wartime pillbox I went, down the footpath towards Crouchside Farm. I kept on walking, not really sure where I was going, but keen to get away somewhere on my own to do some thinking. A fox ran across my path further on as I reached the line of the Old Brook, which crossed the fields.

Walking and thinking. Walking and thinking. That was all that occupied me then.

I reached the sea wall near the farmhouse and walked two or three hundred yards along it to the east to get away from any sign of human habitation. Across the river on the hill I could make out the scattered streetlights of Alenorth. In the distance to the east I could see the golden glow from the much bigger town of Marnham. I drew a deep breathful of the cool night air. What on earth was going on? I almost said it aloud to myself in the darkness.

Two weeks ago everything had been fine. OK, so Cannow's End was a bit of a weird village with its weird, historic ways, but I knew... Alf... and "Miss Cartwright"... and the others on the PCC. It was a fairly quiet place, atmospheric, with good access to the countryside – a good place for a writer to be based... But under the surface there was, I now found, much more going on than at first met the eye.

First of all a lot of weird things had started happening and I had begun to make notes of them in my diary. Then Alf had died, which was a great loss to me, as he was my only real friend in the village. Then there was a new rector to get used to – a woman, and one I found it difficult to warm to. Then Alf's grave was dug up by those horrible animals (I shudder at the recollection of it). Then I found out that my mum, Mr. Glass and Amelia all knew more about what was going on than I did, and now – to cap it all – Amelia was actually my great-aunt!

I paused for a long time and put my head in my hands as I tried to take it all in. A chill breeze ruffled around my collar and a fish flipped somewhere in the dark tidal waters down below me to my right.

And yet there was still more to come...

In the long, sometimes heated, always questioning

conversation with Amelia that I'd had that afternoon she explained to me everything that she knew, everything that had happened, and everything that I needed to know to help me understand this whole affair. Questions produced answers, but these answers only led to more questions, which then produced more answers of their own and led on still to even more questions. And so we talked on for several hours...

Picking up the story from where my mother had left off, Amelia explained to me that my grandmother and Alf had indeed been good friends in their childhood, playing together in the street and coming down here to the river where I sat now. They had indeed seen George Gill and his argument with the River Witch, and the latter had scared the pants off them at the church the morning after the storm when George Gill died. Alf had indeed been inspired by this to protect his mother and oppose the River Witch, and had seen the latter die some 50 years ago now after her own stormy night chanting incantations in Cannow's End churchyard. And my grandmother had decided to leave Cannow's End.

I listened intently as Amelia told me about Eileen's childhood friendship with Alf. Many thought they would settle down together, but at the age of 14 Eileen was packed off by her parents into service in a big house in Sudbury (it was common practice at the time, apparently, to send teenage girls into service miles away) and the two never got back together. Alf never married, but Eileen married a Sudbury man, Tom Carter, a groom at another big house in the town, and made a new home for herself there.

Eileen and Amelia jointly inherited their parents' Cannow's End cottage just after the War, but Eileen chose to stay in

Sudbury, so Amelia lived there alone, where she has been ever since.

As I sat mulling all this over on the sea wall, I tried to picture my grandmother and Alf together in childhood. I was amazed that Amelia had never said anything before, though I could understand her reasons. But why had my mother never said anything? Maybe there had been no need? But now, with the passing of Alf, the old order was dead and we were evidently at the beginning of something terrifying and new. The reason that my mother had been so persuasive in suggesting that I move to Cannow's End was evidently not just because she wanted me to live somewhere "atmospheric in the country", but because she felt that if I was there I might somehow be able to keep an eye on Alf and Amelia and look after them, as Alf had done with his mother. My mother had told me that she had no wish to go back to the place of her conception – she was a Suffolk girl and, whilst she had inherited some of the Cannow's End magic, she had no wish to be involved with it or use it or hear any more tales of George Gill and the River Witch than were absolutely necessary. What she could do, however, as a small contribution, was send me, her envoy, imbued, as I was now rapidly beginning to realise, with hereditary though evidently latent supernatural powers of my own – yes, really! – to stand up for the old order and fend off the new, evil, one that was – is, perhaps – just around the corner.

My head span round as I sat on that sea wall. Round and round like the clock mechanism in the church. Two weeks ago I had been an ordinary boy from Suffolk, trying to forge a new life in a coastal Essex village. Now I was related to a white wizard and being prepared by all the forces around me to stand up to an unknown enemy who was coming to Cannow's End to usher in a new order of Evil. It was all rather daunting!!!

And who on earth was that enemy?

I had answered the question myself even before Amelia had spoken.

"Susannah Black," I had said aloud in that wooden weatherboarded cottage. Amelia had simply nodded.

Susannah Black, it now transpired, was the granddaughter of Sarah Morton, the River Witch, and the very same baby girl that Alf had seen all alone in the cottage on the Halloween night when the River Witch had been conjuring up spells against the church. Secreted by relatives in the old Morton stronghold of Alenorth after the River Witch's demise, she had been brought up to fulfil one aim in Life – to retake the Cannow's End witchcraft crown from Alf and the Gills.

But did she know that Alf was not the last of the Gills? Did she know, as I had only just found out, that another Gill line was still in existence, and that it led to me?? Amelia doubted it. What she did not doubt, however, was that Susannah had somehow precipitated Alf's demise, just as Alf had precipitated that of her grandmother. And what of Susannah's mother? She, it appears, had died in childbirth, aged just 29, when giving birth to Susannah 52 years ago.

An owl flew past me low over the sea wall as I considered all the implications. I pulled my collar up a bit more around my neck against the cold.

It seemed to me that I had three choices: stand up to Susannah Black on behalf of the Gill line, which now ended with me; stand aside and let her get on with it; or leave Cannow's End altogether and go back to my mother's in Sudbury! Mother

wouldn't chastise me. Amelia would understand it if I left...
And yet I felt that somehow I would be letting them down.
Centuries of Good fighting Evil would come to this – Evil would
triumph, Good would die. I had a destiny that had to be fulfilled.
Was I brave enough to take the responsibility on?

The grass behind me whispered something about courage. I
picked up a stone and threw it into the river, hearing it splash
somewhere in the darkness. I turned on my heels and looked back
towards the village, dominated by the outline of the church
towering over the western end.

As soon as I got back I would ring my mother to tell her I
knew everything, and then I would go back to Amelia's cottage
and find out from her what I needed to do.

Extract from the blog of Michael Swain, posted on the Internet on Thursday, 7th October at 12 noon:

well i read sum of the detective novels an proved 2 me bruvver that i cud creep abowt by creepin in2 his room in the middle of the nite without him noticing me an squirting a water pistol in2 his face at point blank range lol! he woke up wiv a start all soaking wet and i woz like lol how funny woz that! an e was like you fuckin idiot wot the fuck r u playing at! an i woz like i'm jus showin you how good i am now at creepin arownd undetected an he woz like well dont fuckin squirt me in the face u cunt an i woz abowt to say sumfing else when me mum came in an said wot the fuck's all this commoshun? omg! an i'm like i'm jus talkin 2 me bruvver ma an she's like well do it fuckin quietly then an do it in the mornin when nobody's sleepin, an me bruvvers like go 2 bed michael an we'll talk abowt it in the mornin.

in the mornin me bruvver woz still a bit pissd at me but couldn't really complain abowt me not bein quiet an creepin arownd an in the end he's like oh stop pestering me u can come and i'm like woohoo we're goin 2 run rownd canowsend church an go back in time an he's like well we better get practising then so we went runnin along the cinder path along temsmouth seefrunt where it's long an straight an flat an u can run for miles an get yr speed an stamina up.

canowsend here we cum!

Stephen Varley's journal, Thursday, 7th October:

12:30pm

After a long telephone conversation with mother informing her that I knew everything and receiving reassurances from her that I would be 'safe' in Amelia's hands, I went round to see Amelia – great-aunt – to continue our conversation and find out what she wanted me to do.

She asked me if I knew anything about Cannow's End church's gargoyles and I told her I had read something about gargoyles in general at Thamesmouth Library following a suggestion by Mr. Glass, but that this had nothing specific in it about Cannow's End's ones.

The question sounded a bit bizarre to me but she was insistent and when I suggested that "surely they're just stone carvings?" she looked at me with a fire in her eyes that showed something of the passion and belief of her youth, and chastised me for doubting the wise words of an old woman more knowledgeable than me.

She told me that I needed to know more about the gargoyles at Cannow's End and went into the back room to rustle around in a trunk from which she produced a dusty, ancient book entitled The Cannow's End Gargoyles. This, she said, held the key to sorting out the current situation.

**Extract from *The Cannow's End Gargoyles*,
read by Stephen Varley during the afternoon of
Thursday, 7th October:**

The four gargoyles on Cannow's End church were commissioned by the then rector John Fordham in 1644. They were based on the grotesque beasts of the medieval period and were introduced by the rector to ward off evil spirits. A note found amongst Reverend Fordham's possessions after his death, written in his own hand, suggests that he was afraid that some sort of evil supernatural force was at work in the village and his commissioning of the gargoyles was evidently designed to counteract this.

He was a devoutly religious man and a strong believer in the threat of the Devil, and often engaged in passionate, heated arguments with members of his congregation. He was known locally as 'Fear-strike Fordham' from his ability to strike fear into the hearts of Cannow's End worshippers and he often took services out in the churchyard, from which hilltop site his booming voice would carry the message of belief in God across the surrounding fields and lanes. It was said that he could even be heard in Marnham when the wind was in the right direction.

The four gargoyles on Cannow's End church were introduced to protect the village – and particularly the church, the bastion home of God – from the evil spirits that Fordham railed against in his sermons. They were also designed, like Fordham's sermons, to instil fear into the villagers that they were not to stray from the path of God. Their designs were carefully considered, each being chosen for a special significance.

The dragon at the south-west corner of the tower has big eyes, big ears, a long snout and sharp teeth. It was meant to symbolise the horrors of Hell – a flying, fire-breathing beast to be avoided at all costs.

The bat at the north-west corner has a flatter face, again with big ears, but with smaller, sharper teeth. This was meant to symbolise The Dark, cover of all illicit activities, and again something to be avoided by right-thinking Christians.

The monkey at the north-east corner has a round face with a sense of mischief on it, plus big round ears and a furrowed brow. This was a warning against mischief and merriment.

The grotesque human at the south-east corner has a squashed face as if it has been stamped on. It looks human, but the lopsidedness of the face somehow makes it look otherworldly. This was a warning against straying from the path of God and ending up inhuman.

With these four gargoyles in place, Fordham, the Church and the human congregation which he had been assigned to minister over, were all protected from evil spirits.

Stephen Varley's journal, Thursday, 7th October:

5:30pm

I read through *The Cannow's End Gargoyles* this afternoon, musing about their origins and the life and times of Reverend John Fordham, the man who apparently commissioned them in 1644. Life must have been very different then. Religion was so much more a focal point of community life and people were generally far more God- (and Devil-) fearing than they are today. Fordham, a man evidently blessed with supreme vocal ability, had been able to conjure up fear amongst his congregation sufficient to keep them in the ways of God. The gargoyles he had commissioned served both to remind his people that there were evil temptations that had to be resisted and to reassure them that by their very presence they were warding off evil spirits. People would be safe in the church building and, by interpolation, in the Church itself.

Fordham had introduced the gargoyles because he was aware of some kind of evil spirit, some supernatural force perhaps, which was threatening the stability of Cannow's End life and the role and authority of the Church. It had been a symbolic gesture but also a physical one designed to have real physical effects in preventing such a threat. But where was the threat coming from? Did one of the Gill or Morton clan have the upper hand in the village at the time? Was Fordham one of their line? Or had he just decided that it was time to stop it? Was there perhaps some other explanation altogether? I needed to find out more about John Fordham.

Extract from *A Short Biography of John Fordham, Rector of Cannow's End Church (1644-1650)*, found by Stephen Varley in the Essex Record Office at Chelmsford on Friday, 8th October:

John Fordham was born in London, probably in 1589, the son of a minor clergyman, in an alley off Fleet Street. The exact date of his birth is unknown, but his father's will of January 1590 leaves several items to "my newle borne sonne, John" and it is generally taken to mean from this that the boy's birth was in the previous year.

Brought up by his mother, whose family had contacts with the Church, John was schooled for a career as a clergyman and grew up to be well-educated and God-fearing. In 1605, when staying with his uncle, who ran a ferry service across Barking Creek in Essex, he is said to have met and been terrified by the Gunpowder Plot conspirator, Guy Fawkes, who crossed the river here with his cohorts on their way to a friend's place of refuge at Eastbury House. Fawkes tormented young John with stories of a painful death at the hands of the Devil because he and his uncle had not rowed fast enough to get him and his cohorts across the creek. This could well have shaped the staunch religious fervour that he possessed, which came through in later years in his memorable sermons.

In 1614 Fordham qualified as a clergyman and thenceforth began a thirty-year career in pulpits in villages in London and south-west Essex, during which time he appears to have been at pains to exorcise the ghost of the memory of Guy Fawkes and his co-conspirators.

In 1618 he married a London woman, Anne Gilbert, who was

five years his junior. She died in the London plague of 1625. They had no children.

In 1639, at the age of 50, Fordham married for a second time, this time to Catherine Curtis, who was then aged just 24, curiously the same age as his first wife had been at the time of her marriage.

Shortly after this, in the early 1640s, Fordham began to look for a new challenge and set his sights on becoming rector of Cannow's End, a remote coastal village on the eastern seaboard of Essex. Cannow's End was known at this time as a bastion of witchcraft and it seems likely that Fordham's wish to relocate there was fired by a desire to tackle head-on something traditionally seen as evil, in much the same way that he had accepted his first posting in the Barking area in order to exorcise the ghost of Fawkes. Never shy to dive into difficult problems and always keen to get amongst evil and root it out, Fordham evidently felt that Cannow's End would represent a good challenge for him. He had to wait several years, however, before the post became vacant and it was January 1644 before he and Catherine made their move to the village. Cannow's End was a remote backwater, with long traditions and a strange, weird atmosphere. It was difficult for any rector to fit into his role there, but this did not deter John Fordham.

One of the first things he did was to erect some gargoyles on the church to ward off evil spirits and literally scare the population into fear of evil. It was here too that he really developed his roaring vocal style, and this was tremendously effective in exercising control over potentially difficult parishioners and attracted unusually large congregations. He rooted out witchcraft and constantly railed against it, and several old Cannow's End women were ducked in the pond to the north of the High Street (a traditional anti-witchcraft punishment) during the six years of his incumbency. With his vocal style, his clampdown on witches, and his gargoyles to ward off evil spirits, Fordham exercised much control in the remote Essex village.

As well as witchcraft being at its height, the Civil War was raging during the time of Fordham's incumbency and, perhaps because of his encounter with Guy Fawkes, who had attempted to murder King James I, Fordham was sympathetic to the Royalist cause. Never one to worry about speaking his mind, Fordham had made many enemies with his criticisms of the Parliamentarian cause in the capital and his strong anti-Cromwell speeches in the City and in Westminster. The need to get away from these enemies may well have been another reason why the opportunity presented by a post in Cannow's End was so readily taken.

Essex as a county was largely a supporter of the Parliamentarian cause, but Cannow's End, a remote backwater, governed by a strongly Royalist lord of the manor, offered a haven for Royalists fleeing Parliamentarian persecution, and Fordham was evidently grateful for the opportunity to get away.

With his twin campaigns against witchcraft and Parliamentarianism, Fordham's period of incumbency at Cannow's End featured many uprisings and arguments. He was, undoubtedly, a strong but controversial figure.

Everything was going well until one day in 1649, when the Royalist-Parliamentarian battles had reached their climax and witchcraft trials were on the decline. Fordham had an argument with an old lady in the village. She was the oldest person in Cannow's End and claimed to be able to remember Queen Mary being on the throne. This woman also claimed descent from an ancient witchcraft family and had seen two of her sisters ducked in the local pond following Fordham's anti-witchcraft campaigns. She was an anti-Royalist too. In short, she was everything Fordham was not.

During the argument, which took place in the churchyard, the old woman put some sort of spell on the rector, shouting incantations in a strange and harsh-sounding language. She promised that he would rue the day that he came to Cannow's End, that she would split his family in half (mirroring the Royalist/Parliamentarian and witchcraft/anti-witchcraft causes), making them fight against each other for centuries, and that the village would not settle until one of his descendants came back to unify the two opposing halves of his family. This was the origin of the famous 'Curse of Cannow's End'.

Fordham's wife Catherine was pregnant at this time and was due to give birth within the next couple of days. This event duly took place on the afternoon of 5th November 1649. Twin daughters were born, but their mother unfortunately died in childbirth. Fordham immediately thought the witch woman had caused it and sought revenge. It is not clear what happened, but the witch was found drowned in the village pond five days later. Fordham was generally blamed and within three months had been transferred to another incumbency. He survived only until June 1650, when his death brought the end of a colourful career.

The picture of him shown alongside was painted during his Cannow's End incumbency, probably in the early part of 1649.

Extract from 'The Daughters of John Fordham – Investigations into the Lives of two Cannow's End Children', written by James Adams, a student, in the 1950s for a university project and found by Stephen Varley in the Essex Record Office in Chelmsford on Friday, 8th October:

I have always had an interest in Cannow's End and particularly in the mid-17th century period when the witchcraft trials and Civil War uprisings were at their height. The rector at the time, Reverend John Fordham, was a colourful character and his life was covered in some detail in *A Short Biography of John Fordham, Rector of Cannow's End Church (1644-1650)*, which I have read and found fascinating.

This biography left one question unanswered, however – what happened to Fordham's twin daughters? The purpose of this document is to try to answer that question.

When Fordham's incumbency at Cannow's End came to an end in February 1650 in somewhat controversial circumstances (he was said to have drowned an old lady whom he blamed for causing the death, by witchcraft, of his second wife, Catherine), he was moved back to one of the many London parishes where he had previously been the incumbent. His twin daughters, Amy and Eliza, were looked after there by his housekeeper, whose role in their development became even more important following the rector's death in June of that year.

The housekeeper, who had heard something of the witchcraft trials in Cannow's End and was an extremely superstitious individual, became fearful of the effect that the two daughters might have on her as they grew up and was very worried about any supernatural powers they might have brought with them from their weird village birthplace. She decided that the best way to protect herself and her own family was to try to return the two girls to their home village and let 'one of their own kind' bring them up. (She was evidently unaware that their father himself came from London.)

In October 1650, with winter approaching and a real fear of having to look after them into another year taking hold, the house-keeper took the girls by coach one night to Cannow's End village and laid them down in the church porch, wrapped up in blankets, ready for someone else to find them. She then left for London and a new life without them, never once turning round or doubting what she had done. The night the housekeeper had unwittingly chosen to do this deed was a special one in the witchcraft calendar: 31st October 1650 – Halloween.

It came to light later that this was a night like no other in Cannow's End. Strange lights were seen and noises were heard in the churchyard, screaming animal sounds were heard in the dark-ness, and thunder, lightning and rain all instilled fear into the hearts of the Cannow's End villagers. The vacancy left by John Fordham had not been filled and the church was under the guidance of a non-resident rector who lived in neighbouring Bashingham. The girls were back where they had been born, but they had no one to look after them. Neither did the village.

But evidently they did have some protection, for when they were discovered the following morning there were signs that several large animals had been prowling around the churchyard and there was evidence from the impressions of feet in the earth that these creatures had lain beside the babies like dogs looking after their owner. The girls were found warm and contented and were taken to be looked after in the village. The gargoyles on the church had a new glint in their eye.

It was not possible for the villagers to look after both girls in one house. They were therefore separated and brought up by two different families: the Mortons and the Gills. They saw each other in the street, but they did not get on. As they grew older they became enemies. They were both attracted strangely to the church and were often found in the churchyard at night, shouting at each other and cursing in strange tongues, evidently imbued with magical powers as a result of the spell the old witch put on Fordham and his family a day or so before their birth. Their descendants fought each other for centuries.

There is a belief that the strange modern custom of trying to get into the churchyard at night on Halloween stems from these two girls, as rival factions return unwittingly to the churchyard to claim their inheritance. The police prevent any access to stop this from happening, but it will continue to happen until something is done about it. The only way to do that, according to one of the many legends about the case, is for someone to go back in time. That person must be descended from one of the sisters' adopted families: they must be a Gill or a Morton. They must go back in time and see John Fordham and interrupt his argument with the witch and prevent her from casting a spell upon him.

Stephen Varley's journal, Friday, 8th October:

8pm

I went to the Essex Record Office at Chelmsford and read much of interest about Reverend Fordham and his family, as well as about the witchcraft traditions and stories of 17th-century Cannow's End. I made notes about everything I learned and I've tried to summarise the key details of Fordham's life below.

- *born circa 1589*
- *1590 (aged 1) – father died*
- *1605 (aged 16) – encountered Guy Fawkes*
- *circa 1614 (aged 25) – qualified as a clergyman and spent 30 years serving in London and south-west Essex parishes*
- *1618 (aged 29) – married Anne Gilbert (she died of the plague in 1625, aged just 31; they had no children)*
- *1639 (aged 50) – married Catherine Curtis (26 years his junior)*
- *January 1644 (aged 55) – took up the post of rector at Cannow's End*
- *Some time around 2nd-4th November 1649 (aged 60) – had the argument with the witch*
- *5th November 1649 – his second wife Catherine died in childbirth, aged 34, giving birth to 2 daughters, Amy and Eliza*
- *February 1650 (aged 61) he was transferred out of Cannow's End after serving there for just over six years*
- *he died in June 1650*

I visited Amelia – great-aunt! – on the way home and discussed it all with her. The creatures that I saw in the churchyard would appear to be – amazingly! – the Cannow's End church gargoyles, which come alive at certain crucial dates in the calendar, usually around solstices and other magical dates in the pagan calendar. This incredible occurrence dates back to the days of John Fordham, when the gargoyles – his creations – came to life after his death to protect his abandoned twin daughters. The noise and commotion that local people heard on the night the twins were abandoned – the night before the morning they were discovered – was evidently the gargoyles coming to life to protect Good against Evil. However, the event had a different effect on each of the two daughters, and they grew up opposing each other and went on to lead the Morton and Gill dynasties as sworn enemies.

Great-aunt Amelia seemed particularly keen to talk about the legend about going back in time. The continuing fuss in this modern day and age about Halloween, she said, is partly because it is the key date in the calendar when the gargoyles come to life, but also because that date has a special significance in respect of time travel! Midnight on Halloween is the only time that someone can go back and sort out all the problems that I'd read about. I laughed out loud when she said that – it seemed utterly preposterous – the inbred superstitions of an elderly woman in an inbred superstitious village! But Amelia wasn't impressed with my laughter and scowled at me to make me be quiet. There was genuine earnestness in her eyes.

Halloween, she told me, is supposed to be the only time that the gargoyles are able to come to life, but it appears that they have been doing so at all the crucial pagan dates in the calendar this year, presumably in anticipation of the arrival of their new mistress, Reverend Susannah Black, whose evil power was evidently growing as Alf's good power declined.

Alf was discovered in the churchyard, apparently having suffered a heart attack; but having listened to Amelia and witnessed her earnestness I now believe that this may have been induced by an encounter with one of Black's evil envoys during the night, or maybe even with Black herself making a covert visit to the village to set things up for her return. One of the gargoyles was loose when I was repairing the church roof – maybe she has some power to free them and got one of them to scare Alf?

If that's the case, Reverend Black, who is descended from the Mortons, made a mistake by killing off Alf before Halloween because there are still Gills alive who can take the initiative and use the time-travelling spell to sort it all out.

While this was all sinking in, Amelia began to talk as if I would be the one who would be taking the initiative and representing the Gills and resisting Reverend Black! I laughed aloud again when she said this.

"You must be joking!"

But I could tell from her eyes and her manner of quiet persistence that she was not. I was, she said, the youngest of the line, and the responsibility for resolving the problem now rested with me. She was too elderly and frail to do it, and surely I wouldn't want to put my mother in any danger? I began to feel a certain guilt about this and the responsibility gradually began to settle itself, much to my chagrin, onto my shoulders.

"Thanks very much!" I thought, but I didn't say so.

I tried all kinds of arguments as to why someone else should do it, but Amelia kept bringing the topic back to me, and she was so convincing about it all that in the end I began to feel myself that I could do it! She says she will teach me 'a thing or two' about witchcraft and magic, which she is sure will stand me in good stead, and also give me information about how to get back if I do take the time-travelling journey.

I'm beginning to talk as if I'm some kind of expert in this, but it's only in the last couple of days that I've found out my own connection with this whole affair. The bottom line seems to be that I am apparently descended from the Gills and that I now have an opportunity to go back in time to sort out the problems. It all sounds utterly ridiculous, but every time I doubt it I keep seeing that look in great-aunt Amelia's eyes. She really believes what she told me, and it's making me start to believe it all too.

Of course there are some practical problems to consider. Anyone attempting to sort this out would have to get round the police, the gargoyles and the time problem - running three times around the church as the clock is striking twelve at midnight on Halloween. The police keep everyone away to avoid anyone trying this. I know Mr. Glass, however, and he may be able to help.

Thinking long and hard about magic after my conversation with Amelia, I remembered a strange incident from my youth which took place at a travelling fair in Sudbury when a woman from the nearby witchcraft village of Borley made a rabbit appear out of thin air. I thought it was a great magic trick at the time, but I'm beginning to suspect now that there was more to it!

Anyway, I think what I'm trying to say is that I'm gradually coming round to the idea, and there are only a few weeks to go until Halloween, so I guess if I'm going to do it, it's time to get some practice in.

Stephen Varley's journal, Wednesday, 13th October:

1pm

After mulling the whole matter over for a few days, I went to see Mr. Glass at his office in Chelmsford this morning to explain to him everything that I had found out since we last spoke. I had booked an appointment by telephone on Monday, and he had seemed very pleased to hear from me.

I told him when I arrived that I had located the gargoyles article in the Historic Essex & Suffolk magazine that he had given me the reference of; that I had spoken at length to Amelia about the whole situation; and that I had done some research into the Cannow's End gargoyles and the former rector, Reverend John Fordham. Mr. Glass knew much of this history himself, as apparently did Amelia, but they had both felt it was wisest for me to investigate it myself and come to my own conclusions without being influenced by them. We had a long chat about everything, and he was very supportive and positive about the whole thing.

After we had been talking for some time, I told him that I had decided that the best way to tackle this whole problem was for me to try out the whole 'going back in time' experiment, meet John Fordham and discourage him from getting into the argument with the old witch. He paused for a long time and drew a deep breath before saying that he too had reluctantly come to the same conclusion.

He admitted that he had already taken the decision to hush up the 'severed head' story in the press and had used his contacts at senior levels within the newspapers to play the matter down. Eager young reporters had been less than happy to drop the story but had been persuaded that continuing with it was only antagonising local people, which could affect newspaper sales, which could lead to redundancies. The police had got the matter in hand anyway and there was nowhere near as much of a story now as it had first been thought that there was. Why rattle on about a non-story when there were more pressing issues to cover, such as Thamesmouth Council building in the green belt or Thamesmouth United drawing Manchester United in the Football League Cup? Reporters were duly reassigned.

Mr. Glass – Edward, as he now told me to call him – asked me if I was certain that I wanted to take the chance of going back in time. It was an unknown quantity, probably very risky and, even if I made it, I might never get back. He told me that he had thought about it himself, but in his position as Chief Constable it would be difficult to keep the story quiet if he went missing and never returned. In comparison, I was a low-profile figure, relatively unknown in these parts, and though the risks were still high, the stakes were probably lower.

I told him I had thought a lot about it and had come to the conclusion that it was the only real option. With all the information I had received over the past few days it had been an emotional time for me. Alf had died – in my view probably at the hand of Reverend Black – and in any case I now had personal ties with this whole situation, being a descendant of the Gills and a hereditary opponent of the Mortons. It wasn't something I was looking forward to, but there wasn't really any other option. It was a golden opportunity that wouldn't reoccur for another year, and by then Reverend Black's powers may well have been greater and a challenge then might not be a success. John Fordham held the key to ending the whole thing anyway, and the only possible way of getting him to sort it out was by going back in time to meet him. This had to be done on Halloween and at least we had a couple of weeks to prepare. With Mr. Glass – Edward's – help and that of Amelia/great-aunt, I was confident that we could prepare well enough to tackle the problem.

Edward shook my hand and said he agreed that this was the only option. I couldn't decide whether I was brave or stupid. He and Amelia would of course assist my preparations in any way I wanted, and he would personally take care of all the arrangements for sorting out policing of the churchyard and preventing anyone – revellers, locals or the media – from getting anywhere near it on 31st October.

We shook hands again and I left for Cannow's End, making plans in my mind as to what I would need to do to make the necessary preparations.

Stephen Varley's journal, Saturday, 23rd October:

8pm

This is the first entry I've made in my journal for over a week – I have been so busy sorting everything out about my preparations for Halloween.

I have spent most days round (great-aunt) Amelia's reading through some dusty old books about witchcraft and spells, including some that she had removed from Alf's rectory in the days after his death and before Reverend Black's arrival. They were hereditary witchcraft documents that had been handed down successive generations of the Gill line for centuries. Alf had shown them to her once before when they had been discussing witchcraft in the village, and she knew where they were and what they contained. She had thought straight away, when she had put two and two together after his death, that they would come in handy to repel the evil force that was coming to replace him, and had been into the rectory and got them out at the first available opportunity.

The books were filled with spells and strange pentagrams and sigils, both symbols of the occult, which were written in scrawly handwriting in ancient faded ink. The paper was yellow, crumpled and faded with age and there was dust and cobwebs on many of the pages. They were bound in black leather, which was dusty too.

I was most interested of course in information about time travel and read up on this voraciously, particularly in one book called the Book of Darkness. It was so engrossing that I often did not go to bed but read it right through the night! With their local production and descent the books were obviously written in the context of Cannow's End, and there were several references in them to the 'Halloween Time Spells of Cannow's End Church'. The hearsay that I had read up about in local history books evidently had basis in fact, as these ancient books confirmed that running round the church three times anticlockwise when the clock struck twelve midnight on Halloween was indeed the way to get back in time. The way to get back home again was to do the same at midday on 5th November in a clockwise direction, which sounded like it might be easier as it would be daylight and there would hopefully be no one around. You had to start in both cases at the western end, by the tower door, and make three complete circuits of the church and be back at the tower door, where you had started, while the chimes were still striking. If you managed successfully to go back in time on the midnight run, but did not make it round in time on the midday run to get back, you would be stuck in the past for a whole year! You specified the year you wanted to go back to by carving it into the external wall of the west tower while the Westminster chimes were striking immediately before the twelve strikes for the hour. The date was always 31st October for going back in time and 5th November for coming forward again. It was not possible to come back on the same day as you left. It had been designed in this way because 5th November was a significant date with enough special power in its own right. Also, anyone attempting the journey would have enough time – 5 days – to sort out whatever it was they wanted to do, but not too much so that if hiding out was required then you could probably just about make it for that length of time. For my purposes this was ideal, as Fordham's daughters were actually born on the afternoon of 5th November. His argument with the witch had taken place, according to the history books that I'd read, a couple of days earlier. This would mean that the argument occurred some time between the 2nd and 4th November, which would give me at least one day, if not two, to track Fordham down and warn him about arguing with the woman. Two crucial things that the books did not say were (a) whether anyone had ever tried this time travel and (b) whether, if they had, they had been successful!

I have spent the last week swotting up on witchcraft spells and jotting down some that might be useful onto a piece of paper to take with me when I go back in time. (I'm going to take a pen and paper as well so I can make a note of what happens to me when I'm there!) The most important spell at this end is the incantation I need to make before the run, whilst the Westminster chimes are striking and I'm carving the year on the wall, and I've got that written down to read out in full. I don't understand it fully, but it's got the word 'Tempus' (which I know means 'Time') in it, so that looks promising! It only takes 10 seconds and the chimes last for 15, so I should be OK on that score. I've also agreed with Edward that he will leave himself a diary note to cordon off the church again at midday on 5th November under some pretext related to the police's recent enquiries, and take Amelia up there with him to wait for me at that hour. This is in case what we do interrupts the time-space continuum, or whatever they call it in the films, and I end up in some alternative reality where nobody knows that I've disappeared and everyone forgets that I'm due back! I've got no desire to appear suddenly out of thin air to a bunch of complete strangers and be treated as a witch myself!

At midday today I went up to the church to try running round it within the time the bells take to strike 12. My blood was pumping through my veins so fast that I thought my heart was going to explode!

As I stood by the door at the western end of the tower, the starting point for my run, and looked at the ancient stonework, the prospect of going back to a time when those stones were so much newer really filled me with awe. They would be less weathered and less worn, since the south-western winds which whip up over the hill here would not have done their damage quite so much. The dragon and bat gargoyles, which looked out from the west end of the nave, and their compatriots at the east end of the chancel would be brand new then – the stonework would be bright and clean.

Those moments waiting for the Westminster chimes to start sounding seemed to last for ages. I could hear the slow, ponderous ticking of the clock mechanism in the tower above me as I waited. I could even hear my breath, I was breathing so loudly! I used the time while I was waiting to look for dates carved into the west tower wall by other time travellers, but there weren't any!

Suddenly, the chimes started, and I quickly started chanting my spell in my mind (I didn't want to do it aloud, just in case!) and simultaneously made signs with a sharp stone I held in my hand as if scratching '1649' into the ancient stonework. I would have to do that for real in a week or so's time. Just when I began to feel relaxed that I had accomplished that task, and was enjoying a moment's silence after the Westminster chimes had sounded, the clock struck one. It shook me to my senses and I was off like a sprinter out of the blocks, round the south side of the church, up to the east end and back round to the tower along the north side. I ran as fast as my legs could carry me. Past the porch, left at the east end of the church, and left again round the north side towards the tower. Three times I would have to do this on Halloween, in darkness, watching out for the gravely path and gravestones to the south and the grass and bushes to the north.

As I ran, I could already picture John Fordham, but I was aware too of the pounding of my heart in my chest and the struggle for enough breath to enable me to make the circuits in time. I had not run properly since I was in the school sixth form, 15 years ago, and it showed.

I made the first circuit and the second, but I was constantly aware as the clock struck the hours overhead that I was losing time. I needed to average one circuit for every four hours chimed. I did the first four OK, but down the north straight on the second circuit I was really struggling to breathe, and I reached my place by the tower as the clock struck nine. Redoubling my efforts, I sprinted along the path on the south side towards the east end as 10 and 11 struck overhead. I reached the east end and was about to round it when the clock struck 12!

I had failed to make it and I collapsed in a heap by the north-eastern corner on the spot where the grass never seems to grow – a full church length from my goal of the tower and with no more bells to strike. I would have to work better than that if I was going to make it in time when I did it for real.

As I laid on my back on the grass, panting heavily and inhaling deeply as I tried to catch my breath, I began to realise that I needed to be fitter than I was just to be able to accomplish the run, and I decided that I should make good use of the week ahead in building up my fitness levels. I could run down to the Crouch and back up the hill again once, maybe twice, a day – that would be a good challenge for stamina. I could try sprinting up Church Lane, as that would also take some doing. I could run up the steps in the church tower – their close, claustrophobic spiral the scene of my panicked escape from the gargoyles in September – and use that to build up my physical and mental strength.

The other thing I would have to do is decide on a plan of action for when I was with John Fordham – if I ever got there, that is! If I turned up out of the blue saying that I had come from the future to stop him having an argument with a woman who was going to put a spell on him and his family, and that his daughters would grow up to lead rival witchcraft dynasties that brought his stone-carved gargoyles to life, he would not be terribly likely to believe me, particularly at a time when anyone who behaved remotely suspiciously was sure to be suspected of witchcraft! Some serious thought on what to do about this was needed, and I thought I would talk the options over with Amelia. I had already decided to minimise the impact of my sudden appearance by dressing up in appropriate 17th-century attire, hired from a fancy dress shop in Thamesmouth.

It has certainly been a busy week, but we have made good progress and I feel much more positive about what I am expected to do than I did even 10 days or so ago. I have been in regular contact with great-aunt Amelia and Mr. Glass, have read up extensively on the background to the whole situation, and am feeling well prepared mentally for the journey that awaits me next Sunday night.

With more fitness and a better plan for what to do when I get to the 17th century, I should have everything sorted. The only thing to worry about then is getting back!

Extract from the blog of Michael Swain, posted on the Internet on Sunday, 24th October at 2.00 p.m.

ok so we've been practisin runnin 2 build up our stamina. we've ad several long runs along the cinder path an we've even tried runnin rownd temsmouth church. i wanted 2 run rownd canowsend church but keith didn't want 2 attract 2 much a10shun. but it woz bloody busy at temsmouth church durin the day so we decided 2 do it at nite.

we tried it first at midnite last saturdy 16th of october but there woz 2 many people millin arownd buyin kebabs an stuff as they came out of the pubs so we gave that up an bought sum kebabs ourselves an walked home eatin them.

we went bak at midnite on wednesday an did it then instead cos nobody woz up then an altho it woz dark temsmouth church is rite on the main road so there woz lots of lite from the streetlamps. we started by the door in2 the tower @ the western end of the church and ran anticlockwise rownd past the porch on the south side, up to the east end, rownd that an bak along the north side. my heart woz powndin really lowdly while we woz waitin by the tower wile the first westminster chimey fings woz chimin wile we woz waitin 4 the clock 2 strik proply an keith woz like stop pacing arownd like u need a piss its just a clock there ain't any fuckin ghosts here or nuffing. an i'm like yeah but there mite b if we do this rite on halloween an he's like well we'll worry abowt that when we get there. an i woz just abowt 2 speak again when the fuckin clock chimed 1 an keith rushed off rownd the south side of the tower showting come on! omg! i showted bak wait for me an legged it rownd there 2!

he woz halfway along the sowth side by the time i passed the porch an the blood woz really pumpin rownd my head but i felt quite fit from all the runnin we had bin doin. rownd the east end we went, keith ahead, me beind, bak 2 the tower on the cownt of 4 strokes, bak rownd the sowth side agin, bak rownd 2 the tower on the stroke of 8 an rownd a third time an keith woz at the tower by the twelfth stroke an i woz a frakshun behind!

u didn't make it he sed an i'm like i bloody did the bloody bell's still sowndin in the air an he's like u have 2B here when it's strikin like i woz, an i'm like well i wud have bin if u hadn't bin talkin 2 me abowt ghosts an stuff! when we got our breath bak we talked abowt it properly an we new we cud do it as long as we consentrated an waited properly 4 the first bell. we woz certainly young an fit enuff an we did make it in time, includin me, i defnitely made it, so i thought i'd cum in an rite this up now first thing 2day as i've jus got up an i haven't bin able 2 use the computer til now. we woz owt late eatin more kebabs again las nite an after that i ad a bit of a nitemare cos i dreamed we'd made it bak 2 victorian times an met the witches an we cudn't get bak an i don't know now how we can if we do so i jus asked keith wot happens if that happens and he woz like leave it wiv me an i'll fink of sumfing! i hope he does! omg!

Stephen Varley's journal, Thursday, 28th October:

8pm

Since my last journal entry on Saturday I have been making good progress both with my fitness and with my plans for how to handle Reverend Fordham when I meet him.

On Tuesday morning Amelia discovered a talisman of some kind in Alf's old books and brought it round to show me. It was a flat gold medallion, circular in shape, with a link at the top which seemed to suggest that it had once been on a necklace. In the middle was a transparent gemstone of some kind, maybe a garnet. It was tinted red, and scratched onto the surface of it were two intertwined triangles: one the right way up, one upside down; one black, one white. The triangles were encompassed inside a hexagon; and a cross, like cross-hairs on a rifle sight, was carved across the middle, dividing the whole design into four distinct quarters. In each of the quarters an initial letter was scratched, spelling out the acronym JFMF. I've sketched it below as best I can.

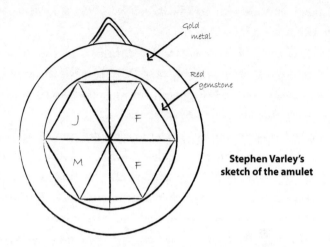

Gold metal

Red gemstone

Stephen Varley's sketch of the amulet

I looked at Amelia in astonishment and asked her what she thought it was. She said that Alf had told her several years ago that he had come across a strange gold and red amulet, secreted in a niche inside the church at the foot of the east wall behind the altar. It looked like it had been hidden there centuries earlier, perhaps to protect it from theft or maybe as a protective talisman to ward off evil spirits. She presumed that this was the amulet Alf had been talking about.

I turned it over in my hand and wondered about its significance. We were both well aware, with the contents of the Book of Darkness and the other works fresh in our minds, that talismans had special significance in old superstition, and the purposeful carving on the red gemstone, plus the link implying it was to be worn on a chain round someone's neck, seemed to suggest that this item might have a special importance. The carving of intertwined triangles suggested balance – perhaps balance between Good and Evil – and the secretion of the talisman behind the altar in the church implied that it had been put there for a purpose, perhaps to symbolise the restoration of order and to ward off evil spirits.

But who would have placed the talisman in the hidden niche in the wall behind the altar? Perhaps a former rector – the most likely person to have regular and direct access to this sacred spot? And how long had it been there?

The lettering around the pattern demanded further attention. We both immediately thought that the 'J' and 'F' stood for 'John Fordham', but the meanings of the 'M' and the second 'F' were not clear. And maybe we were imagining the Fordham connection anyway. We explored several alternatives during several hours of excited conversation, but each time we came back to the conclusion that it must have been John Fordham. He had witchcraft and Parliamentarian enemies. He had strong views and was a devout Christian and a believer in God. It was not difficult to conceive that he had taken a belt-and-braces approach to protecting the church building and/or the Church as an institution, and that he had put up the gargoyles and secreted a charmed talisman in the most sacred part of the building to protect it from evil. It was an intriguing thought.

After my meeting with Amelia on Tuesday morning I went up to the church for my twice-daily run. I had not yet reattempted the full-scale run round the church building, as I wanted to be confident that I could achieve it when I did, but I had been out running morning and afternoon every day since Saturday in an attempt to build up my stamina. To avoid drawing attention in the village to this new-found pastime, I had arranged a varied running programme around different parts of the parish. Sometimes I had run down to the river via the network of largely hidden footpaths on the north side of the parish and back up the hill again from there. Sometimes I had run around the fields to the south of the village and back up the relatively secluded Church Lane, finishing at the church. Sometimes I had run up and down the steps to the church tower as many as twenty times in a row, which was perhaps the most knackering option! Tiring though this was, I already felt it was beginning to pay dividends, as I felt more and more confident about my fitness and stamina with every extra run that I made.

On Tuesday afternoon it was the turn of the 'Church Lane and tower steps' run, as I had begun to call it, and I set about this as normal, away from the gaze of the village. Down the hill I ran from the churchyard to the main road, shielded from view on either side by high hedges, turning round at the crossroads at the bottom and then running back up the hill again towards the church. I took everything at my own pace rather than sprinting, but I felt more confident each day as I turned and made that run up the hill.

Back in the churchyard I went into the church itself. Reverend Black had been conspicuous by her absence since her formal appointment as Alf's replacement, using as a reason for this her need to tidy up some loose ends at the central Diocesan office – dotting Is, crossing Ts, etc., in the bureaucracy of paperwork that human beings so love to create. She had given temporary charge of the church building in her absence to Amelia, as chairman of the PCC and a well-known figure in the village, presumably fairly certain in the knowledge that this old and frail lady, whom Black may have known represented the old order, was not fit, strong or daring enough to challenge the might of the new. This was really a result for me as it meant that I could enter and leave the church at will and there was no one in the rectory – the only building, apart from Amelia's, that overlooked the churchyard – to see what I was doing.

Into the nave I went, stopping just inside the door to look at the rectors board which hung on the wall there, and read the name of 'John Fordham'. I couldn't believe there was a chance that I was actually going to meet him. There were so many different emotions roaming around inside my head.

I went up to the west end of the church and through the narrow door into the tower. Every time I did this it reminded me of that terrifying night in September when the wind was howling and the churchyard sounded like it was alive, and of those terrible creatures that I had seen from the tower roof. I had never been as afraid before in my life as I was that night. The words that I had shouted at those creatures had stuck in my throat, I had been so scared. But now I felt different, buoyed by an intense desire to avenge Alf's death and the need to ward off the threat to my own family that was coming from this evil force. The knowledge that I had personal connections with the situation and inherent supernatural powers of my own which had been lying untapped and latent for the whole of my life had stirred me into action, and I could feel a magical life force pumping into my veins with every new day that dawned. As I stood at that narrow doorway to the tower – once the place of my greatest fear – I was no longer scared to enter it.

Up the stairs I ran on Tuesday afternoon, ascending the dimly-lit winding spiral staircase that led onward and upward inside the tower. Past the ringing chamber, where the bellringers stand, to the bell chamber, where the bells are housed. It was a difficult climb, particularly at speed, but I was in no doubt that it would stand me in good stead for the Sunday run to come.

I paused as usual at the door of the bell chamber, where I leant against the wall to catch my breath. There was sweat on my forehead, and my knees were complaining as they felt the effects of the upward spiralling run. I needed a few moments to regain my composure before setting off up to the top and then back down again into the nave, and I stepped into the bell chamber itself while I fought to get my breath back.

I rested my hand on the great wooden bell frame which held the bells in place, and bent forward, lowering my head, as I gradually regained my normal breathing rhythm. As I did so, I caught sight of something which took me by surprise, and for a moment my breathing stopped altogether as I took in the significance of what I had seen.

On the small treble bell, which dated from 1633, I read something that I had read several times before, but this time it had real meaning for me. Carved into the metal by the maker of the bell, in a tradition of all the great bell-founders, was a Latin inscription in swirly 17th-century lettering of a kind that looked surprisingly familiar. I bent a little closer to make sure I was reading what I thought I was reading, and smiled to myself in that dusty, cobwebbed chamber as I read the words out loud.

"Miles Graye me fecit!"

Miles Graye – one of the best-known bell-founders of all time – made me.

MGMF. JFMF. "John Fordham me fecit". John Fordham made me.

The talisman that Amelia had found did indeed belong to Reverend John Fordham and, in fact, he had made it. I could take it back to him as a sign of my sincerity!

Stephen Varley's journal, Thursday, 28th October:

8pm (continued)

I went back after that discovery to see great-aunt Amelia and tell her the conclusions I had drawn about the inscription on the talisman. She had spent the afternoon digging out a suitable chain to hang it on so that it could be worn around someone's neck, and we both concluded that I should take it with me when I went back to the 17th century. Old John Fordham might be a bit surprised to see it, but at least it would be a sign that I was someone who professed balance and order as well, and even more strongly so with his very own talisman in my possession.

On Wednesday I did more running and scribbled down a few more spells to take with me, and collected the 17th-century-style clothing from the Thamesmouth fancy dress shop. I also spoke to Edward Glass and he confirmed that he had finalised the arrangements for sealing off the churchyard on Sunday and would be telling Reverend Black about it nearer the time, saying that it was traditional to do this (which it was) and that Alf had formally asked for it in writing as usual before his decease, and that any change now would be contrary to the usual arrangements. She might not be happy about it, but she wouldn't be able to kick up too much of a fuss. (We were all concerned that Black might be planning something herself for 31st October.)

The main thing worrying me now is my sprinting capabilities. I went up to the churchyard again at midday today and decided to have another go at a full-scale run round the church in time with the bells. I ran hell for leather and could feel the benefit of all my practice in my legs and lungs but I was still only halfway round the north side when the twelfth bell struck. This was an improvement on my previous attempt and I took far less time to recover afterwards, but it still wasn't good enough. I simply had to make three circuits within 12 strikes of the bell or there would be no trip back in time and no solution to our predicament. I felt like a man who had been sent to save the earth, and I still wasn't sure I had it in my power to do so.

I intend to go up there again at midday tomorrow and Saturday to see how I get on.

Stephen Varley's journal, Sunday, 31st October:

2pm

So, today's the day then, and to be honest I'll be glad when it's all over. I haven't slept properly for the last couple of days: there's so much running through my mind all the time. Things have changed so much over the past few weeks, and here I am on the dawn of something I never anticipated when I first moved to this God-forsaken village, looking for somewhere quiet to write!

I'm still not confident that I'm going to make it round the church in time. The twelfth bell had already sounded before I reached the west tower door on the third circuit round the building this lunchtime, though it was still resonating in the air by the time I reached the appointed spot. I don't know if that's sufficient, but it'll have to do!

I had some witnesses today as well. Edward and Amelia were both there, and a couple of officers turned up just before I started my first run, to ask Edward where they should position the barriers to prevent 'revellers' getting into the churchyard this evening. He directed them to two positions well out of sight of the church – one about 200 yards down the High Street towards the village centre, and the other at the bottom of Church Lane, from where they could see nothing of the church. He gave them instructions not to let anyone get past the barriers after 8pm, and to arrest anyone who tried it. He also said he had made arrangements for a couple of police dog handlers to guard the churchyard itself to stop people from gaining access to it from the fields – the dogs would be able to hear or smell anyone who made the attempt from there. Edward had not yet spoken to Reverend Black, who was now back in the rectory, but was going to do so straight after lunch as he couldn't put it off any longer. He told me not to worry about it and to leave him and Amelia to deal with it.

Barring any unforeseen circumstances – I'm still not totally convinced that Black isn't going to try anything – the coast should at least be clear from members of the public and the media in terms of me being able to make the run relatively unseen. Even if I do make it round within the 12 strikes of the clock I'm scared stiff about what's going to happen to me at the other end. I'll presumably appear out of thin air, running in the darkness in the churchyard at twelve seconds past midnight on 1st November 1649, but what on earth am I going to do after that? The present rectory wasn't built until the Victorian period, so there would either be an older rectory on the site or Reverend Fordham would be living somewhere else. There was a third option – he might not be resident in the village at all! – but from the histories I'd read and my horror at the fear of this ever being true, I had persuaded myself that this was unlikely and that he would be in the village somewhere, and I would find him.

Then there would be the question of what would I say to him when I met him. I had discussed this with Amelia and we had agreed that if I showed him the amulet then this would be some proof of my validity, and may persuade him to be friendly towards me. On the other hand, he might think I had stolen it and might be aggressive towards me. With this in mind I had decided to take a diagram of the Morton and Gill family trees with me, as descended from his two daughters, and if I could tell him that I knew he was going to have twin daughters and was going to call them Amy and Eliza then that would at least prove I knew something that hadn't yet happened. I planned to take a small, light rucksack with me and I could put these things, some emergency food rations and my journal in there.

I would then have to tell John Fordham that he was about to have an argument with an old woman and that he mustn't antagonise her or she would cast a spell on him and his family which would cause all sorts of trouble for his daughters and their descendants. If I managed to do this, I would still have to lie pretty low for five days and then do the midday 5th November run clockwise round the church to get back. And if I didn't do that I would be stuck in 1649 for a whole year, which doesn't bear thinking about! I'm trying to shut all thoughts of that out of my mind.

So what do I do now? Sit here and wait for 10 more hours and hope that everything will go well. I can't see what else I can do. It's going to drag ever so slowly. I might go out for another run.

Transcript of radio message from DCI Rogers at the barrier in Cannow's End High Street to Chief Constable Edward Glass, jotted down by the latter at 11pm on 31st October:

Watch going well so far this evening, with no incursions from sightseers. We have had the usual enquiries from members of the public as to why we are preventing them from having access to the churchyard and have given the usual responses – the churchyard is private property and the rector doesn't want anyone there.

Several groups of youths have been seen roaming the streets, clearly originally with the intention of getting into the churchyard. Groups of younger children dressed in Halloween masks and spraying silly string at each other have also been spotted, though these obviously prevent less of a threat. You will be aware that fireworks are periodically being let off at various points in and around the village – this is always a problem on this watch with 5th November not very far away.

I understand from my colleagues at the Church Lane barrier and the dog-handling units in the fields around the church that all attempts to approach the building have been successfully thwarted. We intend to continue this vigilance until 1.00 a.m., the time when most revellers have usually given up and departed the village.

I would mention in passing that the unusual weather

conditions – strong gusts of occasionally howling wind – have made this an unpleasant night so far: the wind in the conker trees behind us, whose leaves are being blown towards us down the High Street, seems to be moaning like an animal being kept from its food. It made the hairs stand up on the back of my neck. I think I speak for all officers on the watch tonight when I say that we will all be glad when this night is over.

Extract from the blog of Michael Swain, posted on the Internet on Monday, 1st November, 9.20 a.m.:

omg! wot a nite! i went out wiv my bruvver for our planned time travel run rownd canowsend church at midnite last nite as per my earlier blog entries. it was amazin!!!! this is a bit of a long entry but there's so much 2 tell u!!!

we took keith's car 2 canowsend about 930 as planned. we had done all our research and woz feelin very confident. the coppers had blocked off church lane again where it leads up to all saints church and the other road to the church from the high street was full of idiots showting their heads off and lettin off fireworks.

we cud see policemen wiv dogs in the fields to the west of the village so it wasn't worth tryin the central route thru oak way cos we thought that wud b 2 obvious!

we drove past a couple of times to see where the coppers woz and decided to go east an park the car in allotment lane. somewhere in the distance - miles from the church — we could hear excited voices an see the glow of sparklers bein waved in the air an i fownd it all quite comfortin. keith locked the car doors and we crossed our fingers that no idiots wud let firewurks off there! we set off northwards up the main road 2 the kings hed pub. we had bin studying detailed maps of canowsend 4 the past couple of weeks so we knew where we woz goin pretty much when we got there.

at the top of the hill we saw a copper's car parked across the high street 2 our left an a policeman there was tellin off sum boys who woz presumably tryin 2 get 2 the church. lol! he weren't gonna get us so we went east and down fleet island road in the direkshun of fleet island.

in a street called crowch lane which we ad thought was the best place 2 go down 2 get 2 the fields an go round the back of the village 2 get 2 the church from behind wivout bein seen there were 2 or 3 other groups of people makin a lot of noise as they went thru the darkness to the fields beyond. we thought they wud atract 2 much a10shun so we moved on2 the next opening, alenorth way, which was 2 far east of the village centre for most people 2 bovver wiv. even here tho there was a halloween party goin on in 1 of the howses so we kept out of the lite and crossed quickly 2 the back of the cul-de-sack where the fields began and peered out in2 the darkness. somewhere below us was the river crowch. from here the church looked a long way off 2 our left but it was always the closest fing in our minds.

the bowndary between alenorth way and the football pitch – we could see the shapes of the goalposts in the darkness – woz a hedge wiv a big old gate in it at the end of a short area where cars turn rownd. either side of this gate were gaps in the hedge 4 people 2 pass thru. we did just that an set off 2 the bottom lefthand corner of the football pitch northwest past some kind of kids playgrownd where the farm fields began. we cud see the river sparklin in the moonlite below us from there.

we ad 2 cross a ditch at the bottom of the playing field. we then turned left an headed westwards 2wards the church. there was an old concrete wartime pillbox fing which suddenly appeared in the darkness and gave us a fright until we knew wot it woz! omg! i woz like this is a bit nervewracking as we movd thru the dark an keith woz like its just a pillbox stop worryin an i woz like why's it called a pillbox u cud keep zillions of pills in sumthing that big an he woz like i don't fuckin know stop askin stupid questions. i woz a bit spooked tho an i mite have given up then an there if i'd bin with someone more nervous! lol

when we reachd the bottom of crowch lane we woz surprisd 2 find that no 1 had cum all the way down it in2 the fields. peeple woz still up at the road end. they woz still very noisy but at leest we woz on our own wich woz wot we wanted.

we went across the farmland, keith in front me beind, keepin close to the hedges which separated the fields from the howses in the village. we woz on a ridge overlookin the river crowch, wiv the land sweepin down to our rite as we went west. it wos very dark but this was gud coz we woz hidden from nosy parker people and coppers there.

we got tons of mud clogged up on our boots cos it ad rained so much during the day. we ad dark clothes on coz we'd thought of that but we hadn't thought of wellies! it woz also freezing cold. we cud see our breath but we woz after the truth and we ad 2 make sacrifices! lol!

we suddenly heard a showt beind us as we woz making our way westwards across the field. it was at the bottom of crowch lane. we saw the beams of some torches flickerin abowt in the darkness an we thought the coppers must ave heard those kids we saw and cum down 2 see what was happenin. we heard more showtin and it was obvious that the coppers woz there chuckin the kids out!

omg! my heart began 2 beat faster, espeshially as i was nearer 2 the coppers than keith was and as he looked rownd at me i tried 2 make im know that i was scared an what should we do? there woz a suden showt from an unseen boy in the hedge not far behind us and we new the coppas ad got im. we ran as quickly and quietly as we cud away from them wiv all that mud clingin on2 our feet.

we ran left rownd a bendy hedge near a bungalow and hid behind that. we stopped for breath an i askd keith wot now?

a dog in the bungalow started barkin before e cud answer an some1 put a lite on in the nearest room 2 us. the coppers at the bottom of crowch lane heard the dog an saw the lite an pointed their torches in our direcshun. the torch beams flickered abowt in the hedge beind us. we didn't hang abowt an legged it across the field 2wards the church keepin as close 2 the hedge as possible which was really hard wiv mudcaked shoes!

when we got 2 crowch hill pond where we'd read that witches used 2B ducked we followed the hedge again which turned rite and stopped for a minit 2 catch our breaths. we also knocked a load of mud off our boots an i woz like wot we gonna do now an keith woz like give me a minit an i'll fink of sumfing.

we cud hear a man in the bungalow showtin 2 the police that his dog had barked cos it had heard sumfing but he'd looked an there was nuffing there. they woz quiet 4 a bit and then the coppers turned back and keith and i heaved a heavy sigh of relief. my heart woz powndin and i had 2 take a minit to calm down. we looked at 1 anuvver as we thought wot 2 do next.

i saw from where we woz standin that there woz a howsing estate nearby and lites woz on in some of the windows. i wunderd if the kids in the howses were lookin out of their windows for witches!

we got our breaths bak and unclogged our shoes and carried on westwards across the ridge 2wards all saints church. there woz no uvver lanes or groups of kids makin noises thank god lol! this meant there woz less coppers 2. we woz moving parallel wiv the high street now so we cud see the line of the road and we knew there wud b coppers at the east end near the church near the old lockup. there woz lots of plants and trees and stuff tho hidin us from view and we thought we cud make the old farmyard north of the church now wivout bein seen.

when we reached the farmyard we hid behind a hedge at the bak of it and looked out across the farmyard and beyond that the churchyard 2wards the church and the tower. there woz a bit of lite coming from the streetlamps in the high street and there woz sum standalone lites on wheels in the church-yard which a couple of coppers woz lookin after. there woz 3 or 4 people standin in the shadows at the base of the tower near the west door and 1 of them ad a torch on. 2 of them woz arguin a lot abowt sumfing but it was all a bit whispered an we cudn't make owt wot woz goin on an i'm like lookin at keith an he's like i dunno. we cud just abowt hear the sownd of a police radio 2 but generally there woz fewer people in the churchyard than we woz expecting. we got a bit spooked by a dog barkin at sumbody somewhere in the darkness and it made us realise that we ad 2B on our guard all the time!

i whispered 2 keith that there woz fewer coppers than i was expectin an e like nodded and replied wivout lookin at me that it woz still gonna b difficult an that he'd like 2 get closer 2 get a better view.

he stood up slowly and bent forward 2 get out of sight below the top of the hedge and gestured 2 me 2 follow him. creepin along keepin low we made our way from our place at the edge of the field at the bak of the farmyard forwards 2 anuvver hedge which woz between the farmyard and the churchyard. we pressed ourselves bak against the wooden wall of some old farm building and bit by bit inched our way sidewards like a crab does on a beach an that towards the churchyard, keepin behind old tractors and plows and anyfing else that woz in the way to keep us out of sight. we ad 2 step over sum metal fing on wheels and duck under sumfing else that looked like a winch or sumfing. we ad 2 do this several times. it took ages while we worked out the best route and then crept along it. there woz a cold wind blowin up the hill from temsmouth direkshun 2wards us and it made me feel a bit cold and scared.

we cud hear showts and fireworks in the fields to the sowth and east of the church and the village and i hoped nobody woz touchin keith's car! sum dogs woz barkin to the sowth west and i guessed the coppers ad caught sum people in the fields on the uvver side of church lane and turfed them out. fortunately for us there woz no coppas or dogs on the north side of the church where we woz and i thought we ad definitely chosen the rite side to approach from.

finally 2 my great relief we reached the hedge wich separated the farmyard from the churchyard and we crowchd down on sum wet grass at the bottom of the hedge and lookd up at the church tower which woz really high and towered up owt of nowhere in the darkness above us. my coat woz russlin 2 lowdly 4 my likin wich made my heart beat faster and the blood rush rownd in my head like water bein flushed down a toilet, espeshly in those old crappy ones from the fifties that they've got at my school that make a hell of a noise that we kids call the boghorn. lol! we ad crossd the farmyard successfully tho and we woz now at the point of no return! omg!

jus then there woz a frickin howl unexpectedly sumwhere nearby and i woz like wot the fuck woz that?! an the hair stood up on the bak of me neck but keith didn't seem bovvered an woz like don't worry it woz just a dog or a bloke or sumfing sumwhere.

i tried my best 2 remain calm. i woz scared of bein there but also 2 scared 2 move in case the coppers spotted us and came after us. we cud hear their voices much more clearly from our new posishun. i cud hear a woman arguin abowt sumfing, sayin sumfing like this just isn't on officer in sum kind of la-di-da hoytytoyty voice like sum stupid posh bitch from the florists, an a bloke said sumfing like sorry rector but i can't help ya and they woz quiet again.

i looked at keith an he shrugged his shoulders again an i thought well if they're arguing amongst themselves then they won't be concentratin on us and it gave me a bit more confidence.

we sat there quietly 4 a bit while we thought wot 2 do. we wud have 2 run from our hiding place in the farmyard and run 3 times rownd the church in the dark wivout bein caught by the coppers. we didn't really mind bein seen in fact we thought we probably wud b but we wanted 2b able 2 make the run wivout bein caught or blocked off. we woz both fit cos we had bin practisin runnin along the footpath on the seafront at temsmouth and ad run rownd the church there and we knew we cud do it but there woz no coppers when we'd run abowt in temsmouth but there woz here! we ad also practised focusin on the clock chimes and blockin uvver sownds owt so that we woz ready 2 run when we ad 2. we woz also ready 2 cum bak cos keith ad worked owt that if u ran rownd the church clockwise at midnite when u woz bak in victorian times u wud cum forwards in time jus like ow we woz goin bak but the opposite.

i looked arownd the churchyard on the north side from left 2 right east 2 west and bak. i cud just abowt make owt the owtlines of sum coppers helmets lookin like tits on their heads lol! they woz lit up by the lite from the high street streetlamps. there woz nobody movin at all on the north side of the buildin where we woz tho uvver than the 3 or 4 people by the tower. wot we cudnt c from the farmyard tho woz the sowf side of the church so we didn't no if there woz any coppers there. i fought there probly woz cos that woz where the main door woz an the porch an that an they must have coppers there stoppin people gettin in the buildin surely? trouble is we wudn't no til we woz rownd there on our first run an we wud just have 2 chance it an hope we woz better runners than they were!

i kept lookin at the church an asked keith in a whisper wot shud we do now an he woz like i dunno from his expreshun but he sed sumfing like we can't get any closer wivout lettin the coppers no we're here, an is voice trailed off an i woz like wot ya talking abowt i aint givin up now! an i sed oi i ain't givin up now an goin home, we're 2 close 2 give up so no way matey you can fink again abowt that an he woz a bit taken abak and waved his hands at me 2 shut up like he was gonna say sumfing, an he sed no of course we're not givin up in an impayshent way wiv me but in a wispa an lookin at me like he wondered how i cud dowt him, an i woz like sorry i thought u woz chickenin owt an he woz like no but we can't go bommin in wivowt finking abowt it first.

i bloody ate waitin. me mum says i woz impatient when i woz a kid but we woz so close an i didn't wanna miss it an wait anuvver year! keith ad already dismissed all those uvver ideas i had abowt waitin in the church for 24 hours beforehand, hiding in there so the vicar didn't see us, or walkin up from the crowch having got a boat from nearby hambridge village, or even hanglidin in thru the sky from bashingham hill, and that had bin hard cos i thought they woz all gud ideas but now we woz this close that was it 4 me i jus wanted 2 get on wiv it cos there woz really a gud chance we cud do it now we woz in touchin distance! tru, it woz wet and muddy and cold an horrible an we cud b arrested any minit but we woz so close!

i looked at keith again 4 ideas. it woz dark, there woz coppers abowt, and maybe there woz uvver obstacles like lites and stuff rownd the porch side of the church which we cudn't c from where we woz. i woz a bit fearful we wudn't make it and we woz bownd 2B seen by the coppas. we just had 2 try 2 delay bein seen as long as possible, cos if we did make 3 runs rownd the church and did go back in time the coppers wudn't catch us then lol!!! but i woz like still sceptical and didn't wanna b arrested or nuffink.

i looked at me watch and showed it 2 keith. we cud just abowt make out 1145 at nite in the starlite. the church clock wozn't lit so we cudn't use that. time passed slowly like a tortoise or a snail creepin along in me mum's garden by that old wooden fence at the bak near the brook, an in the distance we cud hear people showtin and dogs barkin and stuff. i tried willin the time 2 go quicker but it didn't. we cud hear the coppers in the high street laughin and jokin. one of the men by the tower began to pace a abowt as if he woz nervous. i new ow he felt lol! the lady who had bin arguing had disappeared off home or sumwhere.

i began to cownt down the time in my head.

10 minits

5 minits

2 minits

the blood in my head woz pumpin rownd inside it like air in me bicycle tires when i pump them up, espeshully wen i use keith's car pump that u stand on cos u can get more pressure wiv that!

i looked at keith like woz he ready an e woz like yes he woz. i nodded 2 show i woz 2.

the westminster chimey fing on the clock suddenly started up an made us both jump! omg!

the man who woz pacing abowt suddenly ran 2 the church and started showting sumfing and scratched sum marks on the tower wall. wot the fuck woz e doin?

i lookd at me bruvver. woz we goin or not?

o christ, there's someone at the door now! i've jus gotta go an answer that! back in a minute!

Extract from Michael Swain's blog, continued:

rite im back. it woz the postman wiv a parcel 4 me mum.

anyway wen the westminster tune fing got abowt half way thru keith and i woz like wot do we do now? we stood up and lookd at 1 annuver like we woz reddy. we had prepared as best we cud 4 it and we woz reddy 2 do it now but as i lent forwoods on2 the balls of my feet like a sprinter reddy to run i was amazed 2 c wot the man at the tower woz doin. as the lite from one of the standalone lites shone on him i suddenly realised that he had a costume on like fancy dress or sumfink and he woz carrying a rucksack on his back. i lookd at keith 2 sort of say maybe es bin 2 the alenorth way halloween party or sumfink like that but keith didnt answer cos he woz lookin at im 2. the man woz chantin sum stuff like an incantashun or sumfink like he woz summonin sumfink up like we'd read abowt in those books and i thought perhaps weve stumbld on sum sort of witchcraft richal after all! omg!

we lookd at 1 anuvver amazed then back at the man. the 2 uvver people still there – one i cud c now was a copper and the uvver an old lady – woz standin bak lookin at the man 2 like they woz waitin for him to fulfil sum sort of rite or sumfink.

the westminster tune finished and everyfink was silent and there woz seconds b4 the clock wud start striking. i lookd at keith and i woz like wot are we going to do?

the silence woz broken by a deafening clang as the bells struck the first of the 12 strokes 4 the hour and keith woz off like a shot thru a gap in the hedge and owt in2 the churchyard. we had rehursed this moment in our minds many times but i woz still caught owt when it came. i looked ahead an saw that the man who had been chantin woz now runnin himself and had disappeard rownd the sowth side of the building. i woz wurried abowt bein left beind so i woz like omg, wait for me! an i woz off like a shot 2 after keith and the man.

i scrambld owt thru the hedge afta keith, scratchin me face on the fukkin branches as i did so. keith woz alreddy 5 or 6 meters ahead of me runnin 2wards the tower 2 the right of a large bush fing which had overgrown over sum gravestones or sumfink. he turned the corner at the west end of the building and disappeared from view! omg! i reeched the tower myself and felt the copper and the daft old bat staring at me in surprize as i did so. i larfed to meself ha ha you stupid tossers stare all u fukkin like an i woz killin meself lol! as i turned the corner to run along the sowf side of the church building i saw keith ahead of me runnin like the wind and ahead of him the uvver man woz runnin 2! surely there werent 3 of us attemptin 2 run rownd the church on the same nite?!

on we all ran me in pursuit of the uvver 2 past the sowf door and on 2wards the eastern end of the church. sum officers at sum kind of barrier fing or sumfink in the hi street turned 2 face us as we ran along but didnt seem 2 know wot 2 do. the copper beind me showted at them tho – sumfink like get those boys or sumfink omg!

i reached the east end of the building an ran rownd the norf side. i wud b almost 1 circuit rownd after that. again i cud c keith and the man in front of me. i cud hear the clock strikin 4 above me head just as keith reached the tower. the man had alreddy disappeard owt of site arownd it. it woz all in slow motion like in that film chariots of fire when they run rownd that skool or sumfink lol!

i ran rownd the tower meself an then bak on2 the sowf side

for the second time. i saw keith dodge to his right a bit like he did when old tossface from skool tried to catch him that time when he'd stolen his sandwiches but this time it was a copper tryin 2 get him. i had 2 dodge 2 the side meself to avoid getting caught 2! we reached the east end 4 the second time, one and a half times rownd the church now and wiv the clock strikin 6 overhead. i new we woz a bit beind where we shud b and wiv the coppers on2 us and me runnin owt of breath i cud see we woz not gonna make it.

keith woz obviously finkin the same. abort abort, he starts like showtin as he disappeard rownd the norf side for the second time! an i'm like wot we cant just give up, we've cum this far im not abortin nuffink, but there woz coppers all over the place an i woz like fukkin hell im fukkin knakkerd omg! an i new we wudnt make it. the cops woz rite beind me and keith started runnin off in2 the darkness on the norf side like over 2wards the farm where we'd been hiding unseen abowt 15 seconds earlier! i cud almost feel the breath of the cops beind me on me neck and i woz like time 2 go! an i followd keith in2 the darkness quick as fuck! as i did so i caught sight of the man who woz runnin in front of us disappearin rownd the west end of the church 4 the second time. christ i thought, he's gonna make it!

i leapt over the hedge in2 the farmyard in 1 bownd and followd keith splashin thru the puddles as we headed to the safety of the fields at the bak of the farmyard where there woz a trak down 2 the river. i heard 1 of the coppers fall at the hedge and land wiv a thud on the wet grownd beind me an i smild 2 meself but i dint say nuffink i just kept on runnin following keiths owtline in the dark in front of me as the blood pumped thru me vains and pownded thru me head and i woz sweatin like a pig! omg! i cud feel a hand reachin owt right behind me on me collar an i thought that uvver coppers gonna fukkin grab me an im like well u can piss off cos u aint fukkin grabbin me mate, an then there woz an almighty fukkin bang as i hurdled a plow or sum metal implement thing and the copper behind me didnt and collided wiv it and he let owt an almighty fukkin showt like owwww! me fukkin leg or sumfink and fell 2 the floor in a heap! an i was fukkin larfin then as i lookd bak an saw him rollin arownd on the floor clutching his shin and the uvver coppa woz standin way behind him shakin mud an water off is hands. an i woz like yeh fuk off coppers u aint catchin us now ya cunts! i laughed owt lowd cos i new keith and i woz ome an dry an we jus fukkin ran as fast as we cud until we disappeard completely in2 the darkness! my last view of the church woz of the runnin man in the distance beind the fallen coppers, runnin along the norf side of the church for the third and final time...

keith showted cum on in front of me and i turnd bak 2 look at him still runnin 2wards the river. he woz alreddy owt of the farmyard and on2 the farm trak an we both ran from there pickin up speed as we ran downhill 2wards the river. 12 o clock struck on the church tower beind us but wiv real power like it meant sumfink important woz happenin. the sky crackld wiv lightning and the fields and hedges arownd us woz lit up suddenly like wiv a lite or sumfink like it woz daylite an then it went dark again. omg! i had never run so fast or so far 4 so long an i woz frickin knackerd but we kept runnin til we reachd the river which had a raised grassy bank like a seawall next to it.

stop! i showted at keith pleese stop i'm frickin knackerd but e woz alreddy up on2 and over the seawall. we fownd a small boat there and pushd it off and jumped in2 it and wiv a cupple of oars and our hands we paddld our way as best we cud in the dark across the river to the uvver side where we disappeard in2 a pitch blak creek fing that took us up rownd the bak of sum small marshy island. i lookd bak at the skyline over canowsend, dominated as always by the silhouette of the church, lit up by a firework behind it in the distance. there woz no sign of any1 beind us on the trak.

i tried 2 catch me breath but cudnt speek and keith didnt look like he cud neither so we rowed in silence slowly and carefully an a bit more relaxd an that as we made our way up the creek in the darkness.

when we got to the sure on the uvver side of the river crowch we fownd anuvver trak on that side next 2 a marina wiv boats in it and as we lookd bak across the river we saw a police boat movin on the uvver side of the marshy island in the main channel over 2wards canowsend panning the fields wiv a searchlite. omg! we lookd at one anuvver and qwickly turnd rownd and ran up the trak that led away from the marina in2 the dark cuntryside on that side. we hadnt got a fukkin clue where we woz tho! lol!

luckily we qwickly came 2 a railway stashun only a few hundred yards up the trak – it was called 'alenorth' like that halloween road in canowsend - an i woz like thank fuk for that. we waited there til morning til a train came an then went home as qwick as we cud without further incident.

we've both been a bit scard 2 talk abowt it this morning so i thought id cum on here and right it up properly 4 you witch hunters 2 c wot happened 2 us. we didnt find any witches but sumfink woz goin on an i want 2 know wot append 2 that runnin bloke. we also need 2 go bak 2 canowsend 2 collect keith's car! ill post an update here later if i find owt anyfink else.

Stephen Varley's journal, Monday?
1ˢᵗ November 1649?

8:10 a.m.

I've just woken up in Cannow's End churchyard having found myself lying on my back in the wet grass a few yards to the west of the tower. I thought I heard an alarm clock going off – maybe it was the church bells? The last thing I remember was running round the church last night as fast my legs would carry me, and being aware of some sort of commotion going on behind me. I think incredibly that somebody else must have been attempting the run?! Was it some of Reverend Black's men? And, if so, where are they now?

I do recall that as I ran along the north side of the building for the third time I could hear the church bells striking loudly overhead. The 12ᵗʰ and final bell sounded ominously as I reached the tower – but did I reach it in time? The bell struck before I reached it, but the sound was still resonating in the air as I turned the corner. I felt a strange feeling of nausea as I did so… The shouts and voices behind me became mere whispers in the wind. The chill night air hit me full force in the face as it came up over the hill and whipped round the west end of the church, tearing towards me like an invisible tidal wave. Black shapes seemed to loom up at me out of the shadows on all sides. An owl hooted above my head. A flash of lightning filled the sky. Then I felt like I had run into a wall of water, lost my footing and stumbled forward. The graveyard around me began to spin round and disappear. Everything went black.

It is now clearly morning. I have a bump on my head and the pounding in my heart has been replaced by one in my temples. To my intense surprise I am still in the churchyard, but all the commotion and excitement of the previous night – the pounding of feet, the clanging of the bells –has disappeared. All is quiet – almost too quiet. The wind has dropped and only a chill late autumn breeze is playing with the twigs in the hedges around the churchyard perimeter.

I'm sitting propped up against the west tower door as I write this down.

It is very quiet everywhere. There's no one else around. The stonework of the building looks unusually bright and clean, with a white, new glow about it. There's a funny atmosphere around the place too – something actually feels wrong and I am beginning to feel a little ill at ease. The trees look a bit different – as if they are in different places or have grown or shrunk to unfamiliar heights. And as for the gravestones... there aren't any! Where have they gone?

The grass is wet so I am going to get up and have a better look round. I need to prove or disprove what I fear – that it actually worked! - and I'm going to have a quick scout round before anyone else appears!

Stephen Varley's journal, Monday?
1st November 1649? continued:

8:45 a.m.

I've been to the top of Church Lane and round the south side of the churchyard to the High Street. I looked across to Thamesmouth to the south and am somewhat unnerved to have found that there are no tower blocks dominating the skyline in that direction, which there usually are! The gravel path through the churchyard is just earth. There are no streetlights in the High Street, which is little more than a dirt track. There are hardly any houses. The village lock-up is not there. There is a small copse where the rectory is supposed to be. And there's a silence in the air that is unfamiliar to me.

The inside of the church, where I'm sitting writing this, is the only thing that looks at all the same – but there are no stained glass Victorian windows and no modern pews. There is no electricity panel in the vestry. There are no photographs of coffee mornings and no Velcro display board on which to put them. The church is plain and empty and the floor is made of earth. Searching for confirmation of my fears – confirmation that I did not want to receive – I made my way to the rectors board and looked closely at the names listed there. I could see my breath in the cold, still air as I walked. There was more space on it than I remembered, and some of the names that I could picture, etched in gold leaf towards the bottom of the board, were not there. I looked around for other boards, but I knew deep down that this was the only one. There had only ever been one. The latest entry on it was one that I was secretly hoping not to find. "John Fordham, 1644"...

A shudder went through me as I read it.

"No," I whispered to myself, my exhaled breath rushing out over Fordham's name. "There must be some mistake...!"

But the more I thought about it, the more I knew there was not.

Deep down in my heart of hearts I had never thought it would happen. I don't think I even really believed all that witchcraft nonsense that great-aunt Amelia had told me – all those stories about the Gills and the Mortons... It all sounded too fantastical to be true. And now here I am, on my own, apparently in the 1640s.

I'm assuming it's 1649, since that was the year I scratched on the church tower, and if everything else about the spell worked then it's reasonable to assume that the part about writing the year on the wall to specify when you want to go back to must have done as well. The next rector after Fordham was appointed in 1650 and he's not on the board.

So the spell has worked and I am very scared! What on earth have I – have we collectively – done?

I really don't know what to do next... I suppose I must try to find John Fordham...? He must live in the village somewhere...

Detail from a South Anglia Police computer printout, 1st November, 11.18 a.m.:

The marine patrol and helicopter reconnaissance units have between them searched the fields and river to the north of Cannow's End for the two youths wanted for questioning following the incident at the church there last night.

The farmer at Crouchside Farm on the south bank of the Crouch has reported a missing rowing boat and it is believed that this was taken by the boys and used in their escape. Helicopter reconnaissance located the boat on the northern bank of the river near the village of Alenorth, at the marina behind Marsh Island. Subsequent questioning of the driver of the first London-bound morning train through Alenorth station has revealed that he picked up two youths fitting the description of the two wanted for questioning. They got off the train at Farmford, which would suggest either that they live in that town or that they were changing trains there for one of the stations between Farmford and Thamesmouth.

In the absence of further clues and with no damage done either at the church or to the boat, we are calling the search off.

Stephen Varley's journal, Monday?
1st November 1649? continued:

6 pm

The best guess I've got about date is that it is 1st November 1649, but I've got no idea what day it is. It would be a Monday in the time I've come from, but it could be a different day here! Anyway, the day is unimportant; it is the year that is critical!

The experiment worked and I am very scared. After looking at the rectors board I had to sit down in the church for a while to compose myself. Although what I needed to do next was to find John Fordham, I found myself to be somewhat apprehensive about the prospect of showing myself to an unsuspecting 17th-century public. Childhood memories of the Bewitched TV programme, in which the time-travelling Samantha and her hapless husband had been threatened with burning at the stake when striking a 20th-century match to light a 17th-century fire, sprang readily and somewhat scarily to mind, and I was acutely aware that I would look, speak and think differently from everyone else in the village. I looked down at my fancy dress outfit and began to think how preposterous I looked. I'd tried my best to look the part, but how authentic it would be in a real scenario was another matter! Witchcraft persecution was at its height and there had only just been a civil war on as well, so people would be extremely nervous and suspicious of strange-dressing, strange-talking, strange-thinking strangers.

What I really wanted to do was to stay out of sight and keep a low profile. Even if I did nothing at all while I was here I'd still have five days to wait – and I'd need to eat somehow. Maybe I could live off berries and any crops I might find in the fields. I'd brought some chocolate bars, energy tablets and a couple of apples with me for sustenance, but they wouldn't last for ever! There would be fish in the river, I suppose, but I had nothing to cook them on... The more I thought about it the more I realised that I had not properly given the food situation any thought. I tried to put it out of my mind.

As I thought more about it I realised what a momentous step I had taken – and not just for me, but for science as well. I was probably the first person ever to have successfully used the spells for time travel. Should I set about exploring and finding out things to record and take back to the 21st century? No, sadly I'd better not – I'd got too much on my plate already for that!

It was no good. I just had to find John Fordham. So, risk or no risk, I had to go out into the big wide world and see what it held in store for me, much like a sixth former who's top of the tree at school but has to start at the bottom again, with fear and trepidation of things unknown, when he first goes out into the world of work. I exhaled loudly in resignation and looked towards the door.

I rose to my feet, but before I had completed two strides I received the shock of my life. Footsteps in the porch signalled the approach of someone else! I looked around me in horror and then back at the door. The door handle turned slowly and the heavy oak door began to swing open. I caught sight of the door to the tower stairs which I had rushed through in fear two months ago, and in an instant decided to do the same again. I made it just before the main door opened.

As I crouched in the tower stairwell and pulled the tower door closed behind me I heard the main church door fully opening, and someone stepped inside. After a few moments, I pushed the tower door open slightly so I could peer out into the main body of the church through a hole in its wooden slatting, and there stood someone I recognised from his painting, as if I knew him personally. He was rather rougher looking than his image suggested, but there was no mistaking the scholarly appearance of the one and only Reverend John Fordham!

Stephen Varley's journal, Monday? 1st November 1649?

6 p.m. continued

As I sat in that cramped circular stairwell, staring out through the slats in the door at the man in the nave before me, I could hardly believe that there – in the flesh – was the man I had read and heard so much about, the man I needed to speak to to resolve this whole state of affairs. And yet even though I could see him with my own eyes it was so hard to believe that he was actually real. It was like looking at those old photographs in nostalgia books – you know the sort of thing, *Old Thamesmouth: A Pictorial History* – when you tend to forget that the people in the pictures are real and that they are not just faces in a photograph. This was the same with John Fordham now, whom I had only previously seen in a painting. My heart was beating so hard in my breast that I thought it was going to explode!

He walked up to the chancel and as I watched him kneeling down and crossing himself in front of the altar I was mesmerised to think that here was someone from the past who was very much alive. The more I mused on this the more I realised that he wasn't from the past, but from the present – it was me who was in the wrong time! I didn't know what to say or do, but as he knelt and prayed, apparently alone, I felt an overwhelming desire to get out and speak to him. He was the key to my problem and I might not get the chance to catch him alone again.

I gradually pushed open the tower stairwell door until it was fully open and rose from my position without making a sound until I was standing at the back of the nave watching the praying rector in front of me. I took several paces forward without being seen and then stopped in line with the south porch door. What should I do now?

As I stood and pondered, Reverend Fordham suddenly became aware of my presence and quickly turned round, rising to his feet and turning to face me as he did so. For a fleeting moment I thought about fleeing through the door and out into the churchyard, but where would I go? And I would need to speak to him in any case… I paused, wondering what to say…

He spoke before I could, in a deep, rough, educated and slightly accusatory voice.

"Thou wouldst creep up unseen on a man of the cloth?"

I opened my mouth as if to speak but no words came out. His language was more antiquated than mine and I was scared to speak in case it sounded odd to him. I thought of my English Literature education, and the language of the plays of Webster, Ford and Herrick and the poetry of Milton all flashed through my mind. I needed to answer him in his language, and sought about for the right words.

"Art thou deaf?!" the rector pressed me, advancing down the nave until he was just a few feet from me, where he stood and looked me up and down. Again the authenticity or otherwise of my fancy dress flickered through my mind.

"I… I am foreign to these parts, Sir, and know not the ways of the area…" I said. It sounded like a load of old nonsense, but at least in essence it was true. "I am looking for something and I am told that you can help me…"

Fordham seemed to recoil a bit and then leant forward and peered closely at me.

"I can help you?" he asked, quizzically.

"Yes, Sir," I said, "if you are Reverend John Fordham, rector of this church."

"I may be that, I may not," the man in front of me responded, and I observed him closely, making sure that I had definitely got my man. The nose, the eyes, the hair... all were as in the painting. "Who wants to know?"

I paused again.

"My name is Stephen, Sir," I continued politely. "Stephen Varley. I am... well, my family is related to someone in the village..."

"And who might that be...?" persisted Fordham.

I paused again.

"The Gills, Sir..."

Fordham cocked his head to one side as he listened to what I was saying. He lowered his voice and spoke slowly, pausing first as if fearing he was revealing too much with the following question.

"Are thou Royalist or Parliamentarian?"

I hesitated while I recollected what elements I could of Fordham's past.

"I am a Royalist with a passion, Sir," I responded. "That murderous dog Cromwell should be punished for what he has done to our king..." (Charles I being beheaded earlier in the year, I remembered).

Fordham looked hurriedly around him, put his arm around me and dropped his voice to a whisper.

"Be careful, Sir, around these parts, with such open fearless talk as that! It is good to find an ally, but one has to be suspicious of everyone in these troublous times."

"I agree, Sir," I continued, feeling a bit braver. "One never knows who to trust and who not to, but I know that in you there is a man I can turn to."

Fordham suppressed a smile.

"Tell me," he said, "what is it thou seekest from me?"

I hesitated, not quite knowing what to say.

"Well," I said, at length, exhaling heavily as I spoke, "some of this is going to sound preposterous, but I swear it's all true."

Before I had time to say any more, however, we both heard the sound of footsteps in the porch and simultaneously looked up in response to this noise. I was so unnerved by the sound of them that I turned on my heels and was off like a rocket, running back to my hiding place in the tower stairwell. Reverend Fordham looked momentarily dumbfounded, both at the speed of my departure and at the realisation that that was where I'd come from, but regained sufficient composure to appear unflustered by the time the door opened.

I held the tower door slightly open again and peered out through the slats. I could see him from the stairwell, but not whoever was at the door. He appeared a little disconcerted by the new arrival and turned his back on whoever it was and walked off away from me up the nave.

"Do not you turn your back on me, Rector!" came a shrill, elderly female voice from the doorway. "It is a disrespectful way of carrying on!"

Fordham stopped in his tracks and turned back to face his accuser.

"I have nothing more to say to you, Widow Thorndike," he said, clearly irritated.

"My God," I thought. "It must be the witch!"

I leaned forward slightly, craning my head round the edge of the half-open tower door to look further into the nave and over towards the door.

An elderly woman, dressed all in black and hunched over like the hunchback of Notre Dame, was shuffling from the doorway into the middle of the nave. She had greying black hair, a hooked nose and was carrying a wicker basket.

"You want to watch your tongue, Master Fordham," she retorted. "You would not want any illnesses to befall your wife and unborn daughters."

Fordham looked astonished.

"Daughters?" he repeated, as if in a daze.

The witch continued talking as if he had not spoken.

"Your pretty young wife does not want to be taken ill now, does she?"

Fordham remained silent, apparently still mulling over her earlier remark. I held my breath. Then, without warning, the old woman suddenly looked round in my direction and I involuntarily took a sharp step backwards into the stairwell, leaving the stairwell door half open. I was extremely fearful that she had seen me.

There was a brief silence, during which I could hear the hem of her dress swishing around on the nave floor as she moved about. Once again the pounding of my heart was deafening, and I held my breath so long that it suddenly dawned on me that I ought to start breathing regularly again or I might pass out.

To my intense relief, the witch – for that is what I thought she was for definite now – never appeared at the stairwell door, but the prospect of that happening had alarmed me so much that I decided not to chance being seen again, and sat down on the tower steps behind me for the rest of the time she was there.

"What do you want?" asked Fordham at length.

"What I want," she said, "is for you to go back to London and for my son to take his rightful place as rector of this parish."

Fordham sighed heavily.

"Widow Thorndike," he said, in the most well-practised patient tone he could muster, "we have spoken on this matter one hundred times or more. Your son was killed at the First Battle of Newbury in 1643, the year before I was appointed."

"He trained for this post all his life," continued the woman, without acknowledging Fordham's response, "only to have it taken away from him by you and men like you!"

Fordham began to show signs of irritation.

"I am not a soldier, Widow Thorndike..." he began.

"No, but you're a Royalist!" screamed the woman in return.

Fordham sounded exasperated.

"Look," he said, with a new firmness in his voice, speaking each word slowly as if he was spelling the words out, "I may be a Royalist and you and your son may be – have been, in his case – Parliamentarians, but I am no soldier and no murderer. I am a man of God. Your son was interfering in matters he knew nothing of and, unfortunately for him, became a casualty of war. Now, I have nothing more to say to you on this matter, so please leave this holy place and let me get on with my duties."

"You'll regret saying those bad things about my son!" retorted the woman angrily.

I heard the hems of her dress swishing around the church floor again and the sound of the main door opening and slamming. I jumped in my skin at the sound of the latter but I took it as good news.

She must have left, I thought.

I sat there for a moment, not knowing what to do for the best, until Reverend Fordham appeared suddenly at the door to the tower staircase and scared the living daylights out of me!

Stephen Varley's journal, Monday? 1st November 1649?

6 p.m. continued

"Has she gone?" I asked timidly when I'd recovered from the start he gave me.

"Yes," he said. "Blessed be our God the Lord."

I stood up and stepped out of the tower stairwell. Reverend Fordham ushered me to the nearest seats at the back of the nave.

"Now," he said, looking troubled, "tell me what you are doing here."

I exhaled heavily.

"It will take a while to explain."

He raised his eyebrows.

"I've always got time for a supporter of the King," he said, looking disdainfully towards the main door through which Widow Thorndike had lately exited.

We sat down on a wooden bench and I began my story.

"Well," I said, "this is going to be difficult for you to believe, but I swear it's all true."

He looked at me imploringly for more.

There was nothing to do but just come out with it, so I did.

"I've come from the future..." I began.

Barely had I uttered these few words than Fordham jumped up and backed away from me.

"Art thou a witch??" he demanded.

"No, no!" I said, standing up like a mirror image in response. "We don't have witches in my day!"

I thought for a moment that the discoveries I had made in recent weeks had shown me that that wasn't exactly true, but we didn't really have witches like they do/did in Fordham's time, and I didn't really have time to have a long debate about it.

He moved around me in a semicircle and looked me up and down as he did so.

"I thought your clothing and speech were odd," he said, looking me directly in the eye.

I felt a bit relieved as he seemed to have calmed slightly.

"Then you believe me?" I asked.

"I am not sure what I believe," he said, "but I know the Lord moves in mysterious ways and I have been praying to him to send a sign to address all the troubles that are currently afflicting our nation. Maybe you are that sign?"

"Yes," I said, clutching at any straw that was offered to me, "maybe I am."

It flickered through my mind that the whole 'sign from above' scenario would be a good way to sell what I had to say to such a God-fearing man. We both sat down on the bench again and I continued with my story.

"I've come back expressly to see you, because an argument that you will have with an old witch woman here, in the next few days, causes grave implications for two families in the future."

The rector looked concerned. I continued my story.

"I think the woman you argue with might be her," I said, indicating in the direction of the closed church door.

Reverend Fordham sat back in his seat.

"I have been having a running argument with that woman for ages," he said, "almost since I first arrived in this parish."

I swallowed hard and plucked up a bit of courage to ask a

difficult question.

"Is she a witch?"

He looked directly at me again.

"There is talk of it," he said. "Her family has lived in the parish for centuries. There is said to have been bad blood between them and the rest of the parishioners for many a long year."

"What happened to her son?" I asked. "And what of her husband?"

The rector exhaled heavily.

"Her husband was a Parliamentarian, supporting the cause of Parliament against the King." He crossed himself. "He left the parish in the middle of the night and signed up for service in Cromwell's army."

I spat on the floor to add some authenticity to my perceived character as a pro-Royalist, but the look of surprise Reverend Fordham gave me seemed to suggest that I'd gone a bit too far. I wasn't sure how much to be myself and how much to try to act the part of a 17th-century man. I tried to recompose myself.

"Sorry," I said, after a moment. "Please go on."

The rector continued his narrative.

"He was killed at the Battle of Roundaway Down, an otherwise great Royalist victory provided by the Lord," (he looked Heavenwards at this point) "within a few days."

I nodded sagely.

"And her son?"

"He went looking for his father, but he was a man of letters – a man of the cloth, in training – and he had no knowledge or experience of battle. He was killed at the stalemate of Newbury pretty much straight away, according to local accounts. And this just a couple of months after his father had died."

I thought for a moment. The Royalists had lost the war overall but Fordham spoke with the evident passion of a staunch Royalist when recounting the details of the individual battles.

"And the deaths of her husband and son, at the hands of the Royalists, in so short a time, have made her bitter...?" I conjectured.

"She has always been bitter," he replied with a snort, "but yes, it made her a lot worse. And because I am a Royalist and because she thinks I took the post of her son, she doubly detests me."

"You've got to be careful," I said with alarm. "She is going to put a spell on you!"

He reflected on this for a moment and then his thoughts appeared to turn to me again.

"So what of the future?" he asked.

I drew a deep breath.

"This is going to sound incredible," I said, "but I swear it's true. That witch puts a spell on your wife, which leads to your twin daughters..."

The rector raised his eyebrows in surprise and his pupils dilated to such an extent that it rather stopped me in my tracks.

"Yes," I said, "she was right – you do have two daughters, Amy and Eliza."

He looked incredulous and seemed to back away from me a little.

"Those are the two names I am considering if my child is a girl," he said calmly.

I carried on.

"The curse the witch puts on you leads to your daughters being separated and growing up with different families: the Mortons and the Gills..."

He jumped up from his seat rather theatrically.

"Those families hate one another!" he said.

"Yes," I murmured, "I thought they might."

There was a brief pause while he recomposed himself and sat down again.

"And what happens to me and my wife?"

I opened my mouth to speak and stopped before actually saying anything. How could I tell him that his wife died in childbirth just a few days from now and that he died next year? I opened and closed my mouth like a goldfish. He seemed not to want to know after that.

There was a pause.

"Anyway," I continued, stressing the word in that typical 21st-century way in which one uses it when pressing on with a narrative which has been interrupted, "your daughters are brought up by those two families and it starts a feud which lasts up to my time, in the 21st century, and we figured out that the only way to sort it out was to follow the old legends, send someone back in time, and stop the two of you from having your argument."

He snorted, half with laughter and half with disdain.

"21ˢᵗ century?!" he sneered. "And how do you know so much about my life from such a distant future vantage point as that?"

I paused, suddenly remembering that I was directly connected to one of the families.

"Well," I said, "I only found this out recently, but it seems I'm descended from the Gills, who took Amy in to look after her."

He jumped up from his seat for a third time.

"To look after her?!" he said, incredulously.

I swallowed again.

"Yes," I said. "Apparently so."

He walked about the nave impatiently for a few moments, which gave me the opportunity to consider what to say next. Not that I came up with anything!

Reverend Fordham returned to his seat and sat down again. He began to resemble a jack-in-the-box being pushed back into its hidden position but expecting the spring to go off at any time.

"Well," he said at length, "tell me more about this argument."

I drew a deep breath.

"It happens some time around the 2nd to the 4th of November," I began, "in the churchyard, between you and that witch. You have a blazing row and she casts a spell on you. I don't know what time of day or who else is around. Apart from the implications for your descendants it also brings your gargoyles to life..."

"My gargoyles?!" interrupted the rector, evidently astonished. "The ones on the church?"

I had been so intensely involved in telling my story that I'd just blurted it out without thinking about how it might sound to someone hearing it for the first time.

"Yes," I said slowly, trying to think if there was an easy way to say it but ultimately concluding that there wasn't. "The dragon, the bat, the monkey and the funny human. They all take real form."

The rector had cornered the market in incredulous expressions during our preceding discussions, but he excelled himself with his facial response to this statement. I waved my hands agitatedly at him before he could speak, in the hope that I could redress the situation through further explanation.

"I know it sounds bizarre," I continued, "but, trust me, it happens – I've seen it with my own eyes. I've seen all those creatures in action and I have no wish to do so again!"

Fordham's face showed a mixture of puzzlement and anger.

"How can that possibly be?" he said. "Those creatures are made of stone. Only the Lord gives life."

I sensed I had touched a nerve.

"I know!" I said, desperately trying to keep him with me throughout my narrative. "It's the spell the witch casts. It affects them as well."

There was a silence. I began to fear that I had lost him. For his part, he was clearly struggling to take in everything I had said.

"So," said Fordham at length, "today is 1ˢᵗ November." (That was handy to know, as it confirmed my suspicions.) "Some time in the next two or three days I have an argument with a woman, who could be Widow Thorndike but might not be, she casts a spell on me and it has an adverse effect on my daughters, and that has implications for several centuries of generations of my family?"

He looked at me for confirmation. I searched in vain for an answer that would make the whole thing seem easier to swallow, but there wasn't one, so I nodded instead.

"Yes," I said. "That's about the size of it."

He ran his hand through his hair.

"If this be true," he said, "I can see why you made the effort to come back here." There was something unconvincing about his words. No doubt he was finding it hard to take everything in. "But we need to know when and where the argument takes place. How are we going to find that out?"

I thought for a moment, feeling like he was testing me.

"Well," I said, "nobody but you knows I'm here, so if you carry on with your normal business, I can lie low and keep an eye out. We know the argument takes place in the churchyard, so as long as I don't leave that, I can be prepared and on standby all the time."

"I shall need to leave it!" he interrupted.

"Yes," I said, "but that's okay. She argues with you in the churchyard. Just don't provoke her anywhere else!"

A smile flickered across his face briefly.

"No," he said, "I shall try not to!"

My mind went back to my night up the tower.

"What I could do," I said, making up a plan in my head as I talked, "is hide on top of the church tower. I can see pretty much the whole village from there. If I keep behind the parapet or battlements I can stay out of sight, and when the time comes I can be on hand to act."

He looked at me in a questioning way.

"And do what?"

I breathed out so heavily that my breath was audible.

"Whatever is necessary," I said.

There was a brief silence and then he stood up again.

"Well," he said, "I need to go and do some other things. I also need some time to take all this in. Is there anything else thou wishes to tell me in the meantime?"

My stomach had been rumbling all the time we had been talking, so I was able to answer his question straight away.

"Nothing about the witchcraft, but I could do with some food," I said.

He nodded and left the building. I stood up and went into the tower stairwell, where I am now sitting, writing up this journal.

Stephen Varley's journal, Monday?
1st November 1649:

6 p.m. continued
I am breathing a sigh of relief as I sit here. Things could not have gone better. It is almost too good to be true.

First of all, I have proved that the legend about running round the church three times at midnight on Halloween was true! If only all those late-night revellers who go there could experience what I've experienced, they would be astonished! I have actually come back in time to 1649!

More than that, I have actually met Reverend John Fordham! He's actually listened to me and taken me seriously! I cannot believe it!

The other thing I can't believe is how small the village is! I've moved up from the bottom steps of the tower staircase to the top of the tower to write this bit of my journal and I'm sitting looking out over the village to the south-east. It's tiny! There are only a few houses in the village centre, all cottages, plus the odd farmhouse dotted about. Most of the buildings have that timber framing on the outside like you see in old buildings... Well, new buildings now, I suppose! Will I ever get used to this??

There are no cars, no streetlamps, no made-up roads, no tower blocks or big gasholder thing in Thamesmouth, and no aircraft vapour trails in the sky. I can see Bashingham church away to my right and Pockingham church away to my left, and that's about it! It's all fields other than that, with signs of recent harvesting having taken place and various farm animals dotted about. Astonishing!

I can hear Reverend Fordham coming back at the bottom of the stairs. Better put my journal away...

Stephen Varley's journal, 1st November 1649, continued:

8pm

Oh my god! Just when I thought it was all going swimmingly, I got the shock of my life!

Reverend Fordham was indeed coming up the tower staircase to meet me, but as I stood up to await his arrival I caught sight over the parapet of two farmers with pitchforks standing outside the front door of the church as if they were guarding it. My heart skipped a beat and I ran to the top of the tower stairwell and listened intently. There were two male voices coming up the stairs below me in the spiralling darkness!

I quickly grabbed the heavy lead lid that I had removed to give me access to the roof and slid it back over the hole about 90 per cent of the way, leaving a small slot at one end through which I could hear and see anyone coming up the stairs. I then sat down on the lid to add extra weight and hold the thing down, intending to speak to those approaching from below through the small gap I had left as a hatch opening.

"Stephen!" I heard Fordham shout from below. "I need to talk to you."

I stayed where I was.

"Who's that you've got with you?" I called back through the opening, trying not to shout too loudly so as to avoid alerting the two men outside in the churchyard to my presence on the tower roof.

"He is a friend of mine," said the rector.

"What do you need him and the others for?" I retorted.

There was a brief silence.

"I need to check you are who you say you are," he said.

"Why do you need them for that?"

I felt a sudden 'thump' under my backside, as the rector tried to push the tower hatch open from below me. Thankfully, the combined weight of the lead and my body held it securely in place. I could see a shadow through the narrow gap showing his movement below me in the darkness.

"It is a preposterous lie that you have told me," he responded. "Time travel indeed! You are nothing but a witch yourself. You openly admit to being descended from the Gills, and these men here have come to see that you are put in the ducking stool."

Oh my god! Can you imagine the turmoil that was going through my brain? The idiotic rector had not believed me after all! Perhaps not surprisingly, as I reflected later – it was rather incredible! – but he had seemed so genuine in the church when we had discussed it. I was shaken from my thoughts by the sudden sound of Fordham's voice again.

"Are you coming down, or do we have to come up there to get you?"

I thought for a moment. The lead hatch was heavy and, with me on it, heavier still, plus I had the benefit of gravity, so there was no way that he could lift it off while I was on top of it, and there was not sufficient room in the tower stairwell for him to seek assistance from his companion.

I raised myself into a standing position, making sure that I never moved off the hatch, and peered over the parapet at the two men in the churchyard. They had not moved since the previous time I had looked over, suggesting to me that they had not been alerted to my presence on the tower roof. I took the opportunity of my elevated position to look all around me in a 360-degree circle, carefully manoeuvring my feet around on the lid as I did so. There was no one else in sight on the ground, apart from some men working in the fields some distance off. I needed a plan. I could not go down the stairs. The tower was too high to jump from. But what I could do was jump down onto the nave roof, which was only a few feet down and sloping, and slide down that on the north side, away from the men guarding the porch on the south side, and drop into the churchyard out of view. Beyond the churchyard boundary hedge were some large barns, one of which was filled with hay from the recent harvest. I could go and hide in that!

"Well?" came Fordham's impatient voice from below.

"I'm thinking!" I shouted back, equally impatiently, before wishing I had not responded quite so loudly. Nevertheless, a quick glance at the two men in the churchyard showed that they had still not heard me. They must have been out of earshot altogether.

"You've got to believe what I'm telling you," I continued. "Your wife is going to die and your daughters are in grave danger. I'm giving you the chance to stop this happening."

I winced as I realised that I'd told him his wife was going to die, but the words had come out of my mouth before I could stop them. Oh well, it was too late now!

I had another glance all round, looking to see if there were any other options, but unfortunately there weren't. I was thus confirmed in what I had to do.

I stepped quietly off the hatch, tiptoed over to the eastern tower parapet, climbed over it and lowered myself down onto the sloping north roof of the nave.

Stephen Varley's journal, 1st November 1649:

8 p.m. continued
It was more of a drop from the tower to the nave roof than I had imagined. All the time I was moving I kept half an eye on the two men in the churchyard, but they seemed from their sporadically energetic thrusting motions to be involved in a discussion about how best to handle a pitchfork, and never once looked up in my direction.

I clambered over the tower parapet and hung onto it by my fingertips for as long as I could until I finally accepted that I just had to drop. I fell onto the north side of the nave roof as planned, but immediately lost my footing on the slope and tumbled head first over the tiles and down into the churchyard. There was quite a thud as I hit the ground and I laid there on my back for a few seconds while mentally checking if anything was broken. Thankfully, nothing was. As soon as I was sure I was okay, I stood up quickly and sprinted with all my might – something I had had too much practice of lately – across the churchyard towards the farm buildings.

No sooner had I cleared the hedge into the farmyard and hidden behind some sort of ploughing implement, than I saw Reverend Fordham and his colleague emerge on the tower roof and look about them frantically as if to say "Where did he go?" They shouted something down to the two men on the south side of the church, whom I couldn't now see from my position, and then disappeared again, presumably back into the tower stairwell for an immediate descent.

The instant they were out of sight I turned on my heels and ran as fast as I could into the hay barn, where I climbed up into the hayloft and buried myself under the hay. My heart was beating so fast that I thought it was going to come out of my chest!

I laid there for a while, on my back, with hay all round and over me, trying not to sneeze, and gradually got my breath under control and allowed it to return to normal. At one point I heard some voices in the yard outside the barns and I thought the men were going to come in, but much to my relief they eventually went away again and I lay there, not daring to move, for what seemed like ages.

In fact, I laid there so long that it was completely dark by the time I looked out. I'm sure I dozed off for a couple of hours, which was no surprise given all my recent exertions.

I had eaten the apples I had brought with me during the afternoon, but once my eyes had become accustomed to the dark and I had had a look around me I spotted some more in a barrel by the barn door, just visible in the moonlight, and nipped down to get a few of them before returning to my hay-covered hiding place unseen. I was bloody starving and it was nice to get some food inside me! The apples were particularly fresh and juicy, which was also good because it meant that I got some fluid intake as I'd drunk all my water as well during the day.

I'm writing this up in the hayloft, uncertain what to do next.

Stephen Varley's journal, 2nd November 1649:

8 a.m.

I stayed in the hayloft all night, thinking everything through and trying to come up with answers to the way out of my predicament. I did think at one point during the night about going into the church, but there were flickering lights from candles inside the building when I looked out and, although the hayloft wasn't the most comfortable of places I'd ever slept in, the hay was warm and plentiful and these attributes were most welcome on an early November night.

Reverend Fordham clearly hadn't believed me after all, so either I had to try convincing him again or I had to operate on my own. If the former, I ran the risk of him summoning help and me being captured and tried as a witch; if the latter, I had three and a bit more days to hide out on my own. Crucially, either way, I would have to stop the witch from arguing with him, whether with his help or not. My base in the hayloft gave me a good vantage point for surveying the churchyard, though I couldn't see anything from there that was happening on the south side of the church building, which was a bit unfortunate as that was where the main door was. Although the church tower would give me better all-round visibility, I didn't dare go up there again. There was only one way down if the stairwell was blocked again, and I felt I had used up all of my luck on that already!

So I decided to remain in the hayloft. There was a large knot about an inch in circumference in one of the wooden slats of the barn and I used a discarded farm implement of some kind to knock the knot out. When I put my eye up to it I could see pretty much all of the east, north and west sides of the churchyard without, I hoped, being visible from the outside. From here, replenished periodically by a somewhat monotonous but nevertheless plentiful and welcome diet of apples, I could continue to survey the churchyard until the time of the argument came.

I had been woken up this morning by a general cacophony of noise beneath me and I nearly jumped out of my skin when I heard it. I rolled over onto my stomach, cleared some hay out of the way, and looked through a gap in the floorboards into the main body of the barn below. There were half a dozen of what I presumed to be farm workers there, collecting their implements for the day's work ahead.

I looked at my watch. 6 a.m.

I remained as quiet as I could until they departed, and then got up from the hay and moved over to my churchyard spyhole and began surveillance on what was now Day 2 of my adventure. I knew that the argument between Fordham and the witch would take place either today, tomorrow or the day after, but which would it be?

Stephen Varley's journal,
2nd November 1649 continued:

12:15 p.m.

Well, the clock has just struck midday and bugger all has happened all morning! I'm going to have to get up and have a walkabout soon because I'm getting cramp in my legs and I'm bored senseless with the lack of action.

The rector's been up to the church, where he stayed for about an hour and then left again, and that's about it. I really want to get out of this barn and go exploring a bit more – it'll be a tragedy if I'm cooped up here all the time – but I daren't go out, certainly in daylight, in case I'm seen. True, only Reverend Fordham has actually seen me, but everyone is sure to be on the lookout for a stranger now. I'll go down into the main barn in a minute to get some more apples.

Stephen Varley's journal, 2nd November 1649 continued:

5:10 p.m.

Well, I got so bored sitting in the hayloft all morning that when I went down to get some apples and saw that the coast was clear I decided to go out and stretch my legs. I needed a wee anyway and it was good to get the smell of hay out of my nostrils for a moment.

In the end, I didn't stray too far from the barn because I didn't want to be seen by anyone and I couldn't run the risk of missing the argument. I spent about half an hour sitting facing the river with the barn against my back and although it was a bit chilly it was lovely to be there. Thankfully, it appeared not to have rained for a while so the ground was dry and I spent a pleasant time watching the workers in the fields and for a few moments I was able to forget where I was – or, rather, when I was. It could have been a lazy Sunday afternoon in my own time.

I was musing on this and other pleasant things when I heard the sound of a woman's voice coming from the direction of the churchyard. Remembering the critical need not to miss the argument, I crept back into the barn and up into the hayloft and spied on the churchyard through my now empty knot hole.

There were two women standing by the gate from the church-yard into the High Street. One was the witch I had seen briefly in the church yesterday – I recognised her hunchbacked posture and long trailing black dress. The other one was of similar height and build and looked remarkably similar, though a bit less stooping. They seemed to be in animated conversation. They were trying to conduct their business in whispers, but they were evidently passionate about their subject and occasionally they would break out into raised voices and I'd catch a few words here and there. "Interfering rector" and "teach him a lesson" were the two phrases that most caused my ears to prick up.

The witch was obviously planning something – the argument could not be far off.

I watched them for about 10 minutes until they took each other's hands in their own, as if cementing some kind of formal goodbye bond. The witch went off into the High Street, and the other woman disappeared behind the church in the opposite direction and then reappeared again at the west end of it and left the churchyard through the gate into Church Lane.

I looked periodically out of my spyhole again but nothing else happened, so I took the opportunity to get out of the hayloft for a second time and hid between the bushes by the churchyard hedge, out of sight of both the church and the barns. This was just as well, because not five minutes after I'd settled there I heard two men outside the barns behind me and I crouched as low as I could and as much into the hedge as I could to stay out of sight.

They spent about 20 minutes rummaging around in one of the other barns before heading off into the fields again. I craned my neck around one of the bushes as I watched them go. I sighed with relief at the sight of their silhouetted figures receding into the distance.

After that, Reverend Fordham went to the church again, stayed for about an hour and then left, and that was about it.

I'm now back in the hayloft again, eating apples – I hope their owner doesn't notice their number decreasing!

It's getting dark and the men have been back from the fields, put their tools away and left me on my own.

I wonder if anything will happen tonight?

Stephen Varley's journal, 3rd November 1649:

8 a.m.

The night was quiet and I took the opportunity of the silence and darkness to go down to the river and have a drink of water from it. The apples had been refreshing in their own way, but I was getting rather thirsty in the absence of a proper drink. I took an old wooden bowl I'd found in the hay barn with me and filled it with water and carried it back. That was a challenge, I can tell you, stumbling around in the dark on uneven ground with a lidless container of water! I spilled a few drops on the way and my swearing level went up considerably, but I made it back with most of the contents intact and I'm really pleased to have it with me.

I also found some piles of root crops down in a barn near the river – turnips, potatoes, parsnips – and I put some of those in my rucksack and brought those back with me as well. I've now got a bit more sustenance to get me through today, tomorrow and Friday morning (or whatever the day is this year!) before I have to make the return journey. (I'm shuddering at the thought of that going wrong so don't dare think about it!)

Anyway, there was no witch-Fordham churchyard argument yesterday, so I need to be extra vigilant today. I've just seen Reverend Fordham through my knothole hurrying into the church from the High Street carrying some kind of board, and I'm still watching the churchyard through the knothole on and off while writing this up. I'm also downing an interesting breakfast of turnips and parsnips, washed down with cold river water! Oh for a hot meal of bacon and eggs! I'm nervous about what the day might bring and fearful of what is to come, and especially how I will handle it.

Stephen Varley's journal, 4th November 1649:

12:30 p.m.

OH MY GOD! It all kicked off yesterday, just as expected, or, rather, not quite!

After writing up my journal and having my weird breakfast yesterday morning I continued to be vigilant, knowing that this could be an important day both in my own life and in the annals of Cannow's End history. I'd already seen Fordham hurrying up to the church about eight o'clock or so in the morning carrying some kind of board. About an hour later I caught sight of the witch coming into the churchyard from the High Street. She was carrying a broomstick with her – yes, I know it sounds stupid, but she really was – plus a large black book that seemed to be so heavy that she could barely carry it. She also wore a black pointed hat and cloak – seriously! She looked every inch your typical witch, so typical in fact that I wondered if the whole description of that kind had begun with her – hat, cape, broomstick, spell book. It was too much of a coincidence to be otherwise.

While I mused on this and watched her progress towards the east end of the church, I caught sight out of the corner of my eye of a similar movement away to my right at the western entrance to the churchyard at the top of Church Lane. There, to my astonishment, I saw a mirror image of the creature – another old woman, dressed in black, with a pointed black hat, a black cloak, a broomstick and a book. I did a double-take and looked back across at the witch to my left and then back to the one to my right several times, to check that I wasn't going mad.

There were indeed two of them and they were almost identical, both shuffling slowly towards the church, one from each of the two churchyard entrances.

As I looked more closely at the right-hand one I realised that she was the woman whom the witch – well, the first witch! – had been talking to at the High Street gate the previous day, when I had thought that they were plotting something about Reverend Fordham. Seeing them both in classic witchcraft garb, I now had to cater for something I'd never thought about before – there were two of them! Which one had the argument with the rector? I had no way of knowing.

What was undoubtedly happening though, with two witches, on two sides, and Fordham alone in the church in the middle, was something big. This must be what I was here for!

There was nothing I could do from my barn position, so I decided to go to the church myself. Okay, so I risked being seen, but the consequences of not intervening in some way were even more perilous. I put my rucksack on and scrabbled out through the hay and down from the hayloft into the barn, across the barnyard and up to the churchyard hedge. By the time I'd reached that, the two witches had disappeared from view around the south side of the church. I quickly pushed my way through a gap in the hedge and sprinted across the churchyard to the north wall of the church. From there, I edged my way around to the west end of the tower, sticking as close as I could to the building all the time and peeking round every corner before I made a move.

Round the west end I went, to the south-west corner of the tower, where I was just in time to see the two witches disappearing into the church porch. I watched until they had gone in through the main door of the church and closed it behind them, and then I sprinted across to the porch and up to the main church door, barely seconds behind them. Once there, I quickly knelt down and peered through the thankfully rather large keyhole that took the massive church key that I had used myself that scary night to lock and unlock the building.

Inside, the lead witch was shouting "Reverend Fordham! We have come to resolve this once and for all!" down the nave towards the chancel, where the rector was evidently currently positioned out of my sight. The second witch stood at her colleague's shoulder, staring equally scarily down the nave in conjunction with her compatriot towards the unseen man. I turned and adjusted my crouched position slightly so I could move to my left and change the angle I was looking through the keyhole at to enable me to see further down the nave, but to no avail. Fordham was out of sight.

I needed to see what was going on, so I left the porch and went to the first window east from there towards the High Street to look in through that instead. Most of the central portion of the window was filled with an old type of plain stained glass, but the lower corner panes were clear glass. This was the perfect combination for me, since the stained glass would block out most of the shadows my movement cast, but I could still peek through the corner panes without being seen.

I scoured the right-hand end of the nave and the chancel quickly, but Fordham was nowhere to be seen. The witches were advancing – well, shuffling with an apparent sense of urgency – down the middle of the nave towards the chancel and, as I looked back to the latter, I saw the rector emerging from the north vestry into the chancel, carrying the board that I had seen him holding the previous day. It measured about 3 feet by

2. I could see his mouth moving as he responded to the witches' taunts, but I couldn't hear a word he was saying. I looked back at them to my left and the second witch's mouth was also moving, apparently in reply. I could hear her muffled words, but not make any of them out. This was no good! I would have to go back to the porch door.

I was quickly back at the keyhole, but the witches had moved too far to the right down the nave now to be seen by the time I got there, so I put my ear to the keyhole instead of my eye, and listened to what scraps of conversation I could pick up. The rector was just completing a sentence, which ended "... about time we ended this". The witches retorted with cackling laughter.

"It is thee that is going to be ended, Rector," one of them said.

There was a big slamming sound, as if one of them had placed her heavy book on the table. I fretted about what to do for the best. Should I intervene now, or later, or never?? After weighing up the options – and there weren't many – I concluded that I had to act now and go into the building myself!

I stood up and put my hand on the door handle, ready to turn it and make my entrance. I was then completely startled by a sudden sound behind me.

"And what dost thou require?" came the voice I had heard along with Fordham's two days earlier when they had me trapped on top of the church tower.

I turned around to see its owner, a big burly farmer with a pitchfork, standing in the entrance to the porch and silhouetted against the bright winter sky and the low sun behind him to the south.

"Oh dear!" I thought. "I've got to act now!"

I turned away from the farmer without answering his

question, felt the heavy church door handle turn under my grasp, and burst headlong into the building, to the utmost astonishment of the three people inside.

"Reverend Fordham!" I shouted, as they all stood dumbstruck, staring at me. "You have to believe me! This witch…" " – I pointed at the one I'd seen in the church two days earlier – "… is going to put a spell on you!"

It struck me properly for the first time in that instant as they both looked dumbly at me that I did not know which of the two witches was the one who was going to put a spell on him. I looked quickly and with increasing alarm, first at one and then at the other – which would it be?

I was snapped out of my thoughts by the sudden arrival behind me of the pitchfork-wielding farmer, who had followed me into the building once he'd recovered from the shock of my sudden departure from his presence. I looked first at him and then back at the witches and the rector.

"Who in Hades art thou??" bellowed the second witch at me while I was collecting my thoughts.

I was so surprised that I answered her question.

"Stephen Varley," I said.

She looked momentarily as bemused as I was. My name obviously didn't ring a bell, so she pressed on with her interrogation.

"And what art thou doing here??" she bellowed again.

I thought she was rather rude and I consequently regained some of my composure at this second challenge and pointed towards the rector.

"Saving him."

Reverend Fordham, however, had taken advantage of the distraction of my arrival. As we all looked in his direction after

I had pointed at him, we were just in time to see the back of the black garment he was wearing and the board he was carrying disappearing into the vestry.

"After him!" yelled the second witch.

It struck me at that moment that the first witch had been muttering under her breath ever since I had entered the building, and seemed to be in some sort of a trance. Her companion grabbed her firmly by the shoulders and shuffled her forward as fast as the two of them could go, on into the vestry behind the fleeing rector.

The farmer and I looked at one another in complete bafflement. I then set off after them, with him quickly in tow.

Through the vestry we went and out of what I had thought was the permanently locked north vestry door (it was locked in my time) into the churchyard. There I saw Reverend Fordham lying flat on his face on the grass with the board beside him, seemingly having tripped as he exited the building, and the two witches standing over him, both now chanting incantations.

The argument in the churchyard! This was definitely the moment!!!

I heard the farmer arrive behind me as I stood on the grass outside the north vestry door. Fearing he would attempt to restrain me, I renewed my appeal to the rector.

"Reverend Fordham," I said. "You've got to believe me!"

He rolled onto his back and sat up to look at us all.

Amidst all the confusion, I suddenly remembered the amulet. I knelt down, slipped my rucksack quickly off my back, rummaged around in it and drew the amulet out.

"Look!" I said, stepping forward and holding it aloft. "This is the lucky talisman you made and hid behind the altar – I brought it with me from the future!"

The second witch looked back at me with eyes like fire and I suddenly became aware of the monkey gargoyle at that north-east corner of the building loosening in its masonry above me.

I looked imploringly at Fordham for some sign that he understood what I was saying and would act accordingly. As I did so he reached inside his pocket and pulled out another identical amulet and looked at it incredulously.

I looked down at mine and back at his. Not only was it identical, it was the same one, there twice, once in his time and once brought with me from mine!

"It's the same one!" I shouted, and threw it to him.

He caught my amulet in his other hand and held the two up together. There was a curious ripple around the churchyard as if we were under water. I struggled to breathe for a moment and took in several big gulps of air. Since he had made it/them and had scratched his name on it/them, there could be no mistake!

The first witch's incantations had been increasing in volume all this time, and suddenly reached a crescendo. The monkey gargoyle shook, as if it was almost loose. The rector picked up the board, keeping one of the amulets in each of his hands as he did so. I thought through the spells I had learned in the past couple of weeks, searching for one that was relevant to the moment, and stood up again as I did so.

The second witch held the shoulders of the first from behind, as if magnifying her power during her chanting. The first witch held her arms out in front of her, pointed her hands and broomstick towards the rector, and shouted with an energy that seemed to light up the whole churchyard. The ground shook as if an earthquake was striking, and the farmer and I both lost our footing and fell onto the grass.

I shouted the most appropriate spell I could think of that came into my head, but couldn't remember all the words.

A bolt of lightning came out of the witch's hands and headed straight for the stricken rector.

"Oh no!" I thought, glancing up towards him from my own prostrate position on the ground. "I've failed!"

But at the very moment that the lightning was about to strike him the rector flicked the board over, revealing a mirror on the other side. An electrical charge seemed to pass between the amulets, across the face of the mirror. The lightning bolt struck it and flashed back along the path it had come, reflected by the mirror back into the witch's fingers and lighting her and her colleague up as if they had been electrocuted. They instantly dropped to the ground.

There was a deathly silence.

I sat up and looked at the witches, crumpled in a heap together like a pile of black crepe in a clothier's window. They were completely immobile and, to my surprise and horror, smoking slightly. I sat up to get a clearer view to make sure my eyes were not deceiving me, when I felt the stab of hard metal against my ankle. I looked down along my leg and saw that the farmer had risen to his feet and had put the prongs of his pitchfork into the earth either side of my leg, pinning it to the ground. He leaned his full weight onto the handle to hold me in position and looked down at me in a threatening manner, as if daring me to move.

I stayed where I was and looked across to the rector to see what had happened to him.

Stephen Varley's journal, 4th November 1649:

12:30 p.m. continued
Reverend Fordham was lying breathless, on his back, with the mirror on top of him, the blue sky above reflecting itself in the glass.

"Reverend Fordham!" I shouted, starting to get up. The farmer, however, still had his pitchfork prongs pressed firmly into the ground either side of my ankle, and he held the pitchfork there resolutely with his boot, pinning me completely to the ground. I tried to pull his foot off me, but it was impossible.

Reverend Fordham sat up slowly, letting the mirror slide off him onto the grass as he did so, and picked up the two amulets again. Again an electrical charge – fainter this time – seemed to pass between them. When he was sitting upright, he looked backwards and forwards between the two amulets and then across at me.

"The more I thought about what you said," he told me, "after we had chased you up the tower, when you mentioned my wife, the more I began to have second thoughts. I had two more run-ins with Widow Thorndike and another two with her sister there after you saw her in the nave, and I began to be afraid of being alone in the churchyard – "

"Which is why I always saw you running through it!" I interrupted, partly to explain things to myself.

The rector paused in his narration.

"Where have you been these past two days?" he asked.

I pointed to the hay barn.

"In there."

He threw his head back and laughed aloud.

The farmer stirred uncomfortably above me. "So it is thou who hast been eating my apples!" he said gruffly. I did my best not to look too sheepish.

The rector motioned to the farmer to let me go.

"Let him up, Daniel," he said. "These" – he pointed at the witches – "are the real villains."

The farmer took his foot off the pitchfork and retracted the latter from the ground, freeing up my leg, which I then rubbed a little because it was quite sore where the pitchfork had been pressed into it. The Reverend rose to his feet and then helped me to mine. All three of us walked over to the pile of smouldering clothing.

As we stood there, looking at them, trying to make out bodies in the pile, the black clothes seemed to deflate from the inside, and flattened themselves to the ground. All that was left were cloaks, hats, dresses and broomsticks. The bodies of the witches were gone!

I looked at Reverend Fordham for an explanation.

"You have not encountered this before then?" he said, matter-of-factly, reading the incredulity in my eyes.

"No..." I muttered, musing thoughtfully over the possibility that this was a common occurrence here.

The rector looked at Daniel.

"Leave it to me," said the farmer, as if replying to a question which the rector had not asked.

"Come," said Reverend Fordham gently, ushering me towards the vestry door. "Tell me more about the future."

Stephen Varley's journal, 4th November 1649:

12:30 p.m. continued

I'm sitting here writing up yesterday's events in an upstairs room at the Reverend's house. We spent a couple of hours in the church talking everything over. We talked about my time, his time, our family histories, the witches, everything. By the time we'd come out of the building, the farmer and the witches' clothing had gone. The only thing left to show that anything had happened was a bare patch of grass where the witches had lain – the spot in the churchyard where we could never get anything to grow!

A small crowd had gathered at the church gate in the High Street as word had got round, and I felt a bit like a celebrity as Reverend Fordham shepherded me through them. Nobody spoke, but there were general murmurings of what seemed to be approbation, and I took it that they were thanking us for what we had done. Reverend Fordham nodded at selected individuals and shook hands with others. I copied his behaviour and did the same, despite not knowing any of the individuals in question!

Once through the crowd we left them behind us and went to the 'Stag' public house, where we were welcomed by the landlord with such enthusiasm and deference that we could have been royalty. The crowd we had walked through appeared after a polite interval and, as the drink began to flow and the music to play, there was a real party atmosphere in the inn throughout the rest of the day. For the first time since my arrival in 1649 I began to feel relaxed and welcome. People slapped me on the back and brought me so many jugs full of ale that the whole scene soon began to become blurry. There was music and dancing and laughter and joy for hours and hours and hours on end.

I woke up with a massive hangover. I was lying on my back on a bed in a strange bedroom, which turned out to be the upstairs in the rector's cottage in the High Street. It looked vaguely familiar, and I finally realised that it was great-aunt Amelia's cottage in my time! The room was spinning and I felt quite sick. I turned my head, wincing at the pounding bloodflow that was coursing through it as I did so, and looked out of the window, which faced the church. After lying semi-conscious in that state for some period of time, I managed, after considerable effort, to get up out of bed, walk across the room and open the door to the landing, holding my hand to my head as I did so in a failed attempt to stop the pounding, and crept out with the intention of exploring my surroundings without waking any other occupants.

As I stepped onto the landing, however, the wooden floorboards creaked under my weight and I stopped suddenly at the sound of movement downstairs.

"You are awake then, Master Stephen?!" came Reverend Fordham's voice up the narrow, wooden stairway. "Come down for some breakfast."

I followed these instructions, slowly, mechanically, automatically, and found myself in the warm kitchen where I had often been entertained by Amelia. The electric fire had gone, to be replaced, or rather preceded, by a roaring fire. The rector was seated at a table, being served his breakfast by what I took to be his housekeeper. His heavily pregnant wife sat in a corner with an expression of tiredness and mild pain on her face.

I said good morning to the rector and nodded to the ladies, and responded to the invitation he made with the motion of his hand to sit at a second place setting, which had evidently been set up in expectation of my arrival.

The rector looked me up and down as I sat there holding my head in my hands.

"Too much ale?" he asked, smiling broadly and already knowing the answer.

I couldn't bear to speak, so I nodded.

He laughed.

"Take some of this for sustenance," he said, motioning his housekeeper to put what looked like a plate of hot porridge in front of me. "Your headache will soon wear off."

The morning seemed to pass with me sitting silently at the table, his wife sitting silently in the corner, and the rector and his housekeeper moving in slow motion around us as they attended to a hundred and one different tasks. It took me until about 11:30 a.m. before I started to feel my head clearing and I gave them my leave, as if in a dream, and returned to my room, where I began to write up this diary.

If my calculations are correct it is now 12:30 p.m. on 4th November and I have got less than 24 hours before taking my trip "back to the future", as Marty McFly from the film of that name might have said. I'll give it another hour so my head can clear and then I'll go and find the rector and make the arrangements for the journey.

Stephen Varley's journal, 4th November 1649 (continued):

11:30 p.m.

Well, apart from feeling hungover, I had an enjoyable after-noon. Reverend Fordham took me around the parish and it was nice to be able to spend some time there without being cooped up in the barn! The few people we bumped into doffed their caps to me or curtsied. I felt like some sort of distinguished visitor!

It was weird walking around the place really. The lie of the land was the same, but there were trees in places they shouldn't have been, or missing from places they should. There were no pave-ments, no cars, no street lighting. Huge estates of housing were missing, and the roads were not made up. There were no aircraft vapour trails in the sky. There was no machinery of any kind visible anywhere. I felt strangely relaxed about this, like I was somehow more in contact with Nature, without all the man-made accoutrements of post-18th century industrial Britain.

We looked south towards Thamesmouth (there was no Thamesmouth in existence in 1649, of course, it being an 18th-century creation) and north across the Crouch to Marnham, and there was hardly any development anywhere. There was lots of river traffic (all wind-powered), there were farm carts, there were men working in the fields. It was all a much simpler, much more natural lifestyle from the hectic one I had left behind a few days earlier, and there was something about it that made me think for more than a few moments about staying.

But I guessed it was a hard life too. The work in the fields looked back-breaking, and finding meals for oneself, as I had discovered in the barn, was a much greater challenge than just popping to the nearest supermarket or takeaway. I felt privileged to have glimpsed this lost world first hand, but I didn't think I could stay there long term – it was out of my time and I was alien to it. It did, however, give me a hankering to move again to some even more remote or rural place – Cornwall perhaps, or Northumberland, or the Scottish Highlands.

When it got dark, the rector and I finished our perambulation and went back to his cottage, where we spent a pleasant evening chatting about everything under the sun. I had told him about the need for me to journey back to my time by running clockwise at midday around the church, and he agreed to accompany me to the church and stay with me to see me off. He tried his best to be reassuring but for all we knew no one had attempted it before, and I was VERY nervous! I came up to bed around 10 p.m. and I've been trying to sleep without success ever since, so I decided to get up and write up this diary.

Stephen Varley's journal, 5th November 1649:

11:30 a.m.

After a fitful night's sleep I got up feeling completely unrefreshed – I might as well not have gone to bed at all. I did my best to eat the hearty breakfast Reverend Fordham's housekeeper had gone to the trouble of preparing, but I felt sick to the pit of my stomach just at the thought of the midday run ahead of me and I struggled to get it down without making myself feel sick. Reverend Fordham evidently picked this up and tried various methods of distracting me, including talking about the weather, farming and the service he was preparing for Sunday, but all to no avail. It just went in one ear and out the other.

I said a final goodbye to his imminently due wife and attentive housekeeper and went for a brisk walk round the village again, on my own this time, taking as much of it in as I could. However, I was petrified about missing my time-travelling window, and came up to the church so early that the clock was striking 10 when I entered the churchyard through the gate from the High Street. I'm sitting in the porch now, writing this up – I hope it will be my last 1649 entry! Time has been dragging, but I've done everything I can think of to kill it, including making two preparatory three-circuit runs around the church – clockwise this time – to get myself ready for the real one. I made the first run at about 10:30-ish and the second one on the chimes for 11 o'clock. I just about made both okay, which I found reassuring. It was odd going clockwise though – I had never practised that at all back home – well, here actually, but in the future! There are bushes in different places, but the structure of the church is the same and there will be no gravestones or policemen to avoid. It will also be daylight, which is a tremendous help! I've found a suitable stone to mark my year of return onto the tower wall with, so I think that's everything covered.

While I'm writing this, I can see Reverend Fordham coming out of his cottage, so I'll sign off here for now. Hopefully the next time I write in this journal I will be back in my own time! And what a welcome relief that will be!

**Transcript of a radio message from
The Chief Constable of South Anglia Police,
Edward Glass, to DCI Rogers, Cannow's End,
Friday, 5th November, 12.37 p.m.**

Detective Chief Inspector,
The operation at Cannow's End church has been completed. You can tell your men to stand down.
Chief Constable Glass

Extract from the blog of Michael Swain, posted on the Internet on Friday, 5th November at 4.30 p.m.

hello fellow witchunters! unfortunately this will b my last entry in my blog. the fukkin coppers came rownd this mornin an told me theyd read it and were none 2 happy that keith an i had run rownd canowsend church on halloween and told us 2 take the blog down. theyve given us til midnite 2 do it. we woz both cautiond and told not 2 go 2 canowsend on halloween again. omg! bastards! i thought i'd put this entry on here 2 tell them how I felt – they can fuck off! cunts!

anyway, keith sez i'd better delete it all so i'll do it 2nite when we've cum bak from our frends fireworks party. me mum says that a cousin she didnt know she had has just turnd up at the door out of the blue so we're taking her 2. great!

well it woz all a bit of an adventure i suppose, but ultimately halloween woz a bit of a fiasco and i'm very disappointed we never saw any witches. lets hope November the fifth is better.

end of blog, i suppose. 4 now...

Stephen Varley's journal, Friday, 5th November:

8 p.m.

Well, I shall sleep very soundly tonight! Thankfully, everything went well and I'm back! I feel very tired from the last few days' exertions but I cannot tell you how glad I am to have made it there and back again in one piece!

I was so nervous waiting for the Westminster chimes at lunchtime, that as soon as the first note struck I wrote the year on the wall at the most rapid pace I could muster. Great-aunt Amelia told me that she and Mr. Glass knew that I was coming back the minute they saw it appear. They had been worrying since Sunday about whether or not I had made it. All they knew for certain was that at the twelfth stroke of the clock at midnight on Halloween I had disappeared into thin air! Whether I had made it to 1649; whether, once I'd got there, I had been able to complete my mission; and whether or not I was able to get back again after I'd carried it out were all unknown to them. The appearance of the writing on the tower as the chimes started was the first evidence they had had that I was still alive! Edward's diary note had evidently worked!

They stood patiently waiting for me with their backs to the west door of the tower while the clock struck 12 overhead, and when I appeared from behind the south side of the church to their left they immediately came over to greet me. For my part, I collapsed in a heap on the grass from both physical and mental exhaustion. Thankfully, Mr. Glass, ever prepared, had arranged for some first-aiders to be on hand just in case, and they soon had me sitting up and drinking some medicinal cure-all.

I can't tell you how relieved I was to see Amelia's and Edward's faces! It was confirmation for me that I was back, safe and sound at last after my adventure. I was even more delighted and surprised to see the world's most beautiful minutes' secretary there, especially when she started hugging me and telling me she loved me!

"Aren't you going to kiss your wife?" asked great-aunt Amelia.

"My wife?!" I thought, but somehow managed not to say it aloud.

I looked at Sophie's ring finger and saw that she had a ring on, and as she held my hands in hers I noticed that I had one on too, and that the rings were of matching designs! Beautiful Sophie my wife?? I always knew there was a God!

We all went off to Amelia's cottage – Sophie hand in hand with me, and me completely overwhelmed by it all. I found entering Amelia's cottage to be a rather bizarre experience since not half an hour earlier I had seen John Fordham coming out of it! As we went in I began to notice little differences – decor, kitchen units, television etc. – between then and now, and had trouble taking it all in. And blow me down with a feather, I almost collapsed on the floor when who should I find sitting in one of Amelia's armchairs but dear old Alf, alive and well and smiling at me. It brought tears of astonishment and joy to my eyes, and I went straight over to him and hugged him with all the passion of a mother welcoming her feared-dead son back home from the fields of Flanders in the First World War! I'm crying about it now as I write this. I could not believe he was still alive. Thank God for the time-space continuum!

After I'd recovered my composure and was clearly safe to be

left in the care of one person, Edward, Amelia and Alf went back to the church for half an hour to tidy up and left Sophie and me in the cottage to have some time together. We just made idle chitchat really – I was still struggling to comprehend that I was married to Sophie, and didn't know what to say.

"Are you OK, Darling?" she asked at one point. "I was worried I might have lost you for ever."

"I'm fabulous, Sophie," I said, risking a quick kiss on her nose.

She kissed me full on the lips in return.

Tears of joy welled up in my eyes.

"You're bound to be emotional, Darling," she said. "You've been on a bit of a journey."

All I could do was nod in reply. Clearly my adventure with John Fordham was over, but a new one with a new wife was about to begin!

When Edward and Amelia returned we all sat in the kitchen where I had breakfast with the rector just this morning, and I told them everything that had happened. Amelia told me that Reverend Black, who had moved into the village on Monday and had been scheduled to succeed Alf, who had officially retired, had not been seen at all since yesterday, and that when Edward had knocked on the rectory door to tell her about lunchtime's police operation he had received no answer.

She also showed me a copy of a glossy colour booklet which looked like it had been printed in the 1960s and was showing its age, with faded colours and curled edges. It had been paid for by a subscription from Cannow's End villagers and celebrated the life of "Cannow's End's most beloved incumbent" Bishop John Fordham! There was a picture inside the front cover of Fordham in bishop's regalia, and the caption to the picture read "A painting of Bishop John Fordham in 1669, which was commissioned to commemorate the 25th anniversary of his incumbency at Cannow's End in Essex". I had to do a double-take of the 'Bishop', but it was definitely him. And 1669! Before I left he had died in 1650, so he obviously got some extra years out of our adventure as well.

Amelia was particularly keen to show me another picture a few pages into the book. It was a painting of Bishop Fordham's wife, twin daughters and a hitherto unknown son called Stephen! I nearly choked on my tea!

"Where did you get this book from?" I asked.

"I found it on the altar just now while Edward and I were tidying up," she replied. "I've got no idea how it got there - I've never seen it before in my life!"

As I flicked through the booklet, a loose sheet of faded, ageing paper fell out, and I was astonished when I bent down to pick it up and started to read it.

"Dear Stephen," it read. "Thank you for all your help. Sorry I doubted you."

It was signed "Bishop John".

I couldn't believe it! Good old Fordham!

Apart from these astonishing initial discoveries, everything else appeared as normal. When I looked over the church building later, lingering for ages at the rectors board, which now showed Bishop Fordham in a longer and evidently much more prosperous incumbency than had been recorded on there previously, I was greatly reassured to see that the gargoyles on the outside of the structure were solidly in their places. The church stood strong and tall as ever, and there was a feeling of calm over the village as it bathed in the bright, late autumn sunshine.

Letter from the Diocesan Office in Thamesmouth to Miss Amelia Cartwright, Friday, 26th November

Dear Miss Cartwright,

I write in reply to your letter of 23rd November about Reverend Susannah Black, the intended successor to Reverend Park as incumbent at Cannow's End church.

I regret to report that nothing has been seen or heard of Reverend Black since 4th November. She is not answering her phone and the rectory appears to be empty. We have reported her disappearance to Chief Constable Glass, who has confirmed that his men are investigating.

Please be assured that in Reverend Black's absence a new rector will be appointed at Cannow's End. I expect him to take up position before Christmas (I currently have 21st December pencilled in) to ensure that the needs of the parishioners there are properly administered to.

Yours sincerely,

Roger Partridge, Diocesan Officer

Stephen Varley's journal, Friday, 7th January:

1 p.m.

I enjoyed a great Christmas with Sophie at Mum's and Dad's in Sudbury, laughing, joking and generally relaxing more than I've done for some considerable time. Even great-aunt Amelia was there. She told me that a new Cannow's End rector, Reverend Brian Grant, had been appointed and was settling in nicely and seemed quite normal. She called him on the phone from my parents' house and I spoke to him briefly myself. He sounded like a really nice guy.

I left my Cannow's End house when the lease ran out last week and I'm currently writing this journal up in a pub in Northumberland, looking out over a vast expanse of wild but untouched countryside. Sophie and I have just been looking round a house we like – remote, quiet, rural. I wonder what its history is like? We're going to put in an offer for it this afternoon.

At last the Curse of Cannow's End is behind me, and I can settle into a new life with my new wife in this remote and quiet area of the country. I've started writing my novel again, and I've got plenty of new ideas for it too…!

THE END